STEVE NEWLIN'S

FIELD GUIDE TO VAMPIRES

(AND OTHER CREATURES OF SATAN)

STEVE NEW

FIELD G
TO VAMP

(AND OTHER CREATURES OF SATAN)

STEVE,
FOUND THIS RELIC FROM YOUR PAST LIFE. THOUGHT YOU MIGHT LIKE IT BACK.
PAM AND I MADE SOME . . . MINOR CORRECTIONS.
-E. NORTHMAN

GIANNA SOBOL and MICHAEL MCMILLIAN

CHRONICLE BOOKS
SAN FRANCISCO

Eric,

When was the last time you were amused? Like truly and deeply tickled pink? Over my last hundred years as a vampire, I can probably count the times I've experienced this "feeling" on one finger. (If you think I'm referring to the blonde, leggy Cape Cod twins we drained back in the 1970s, you're absofuckinglutely right).

DON'T TELL ME YOU'VE FORGOTTEN ABOUT THE TIME WE GOT DOWN WITH THOSE SUFFRAGETTES IN 1920 BROOKLYN. IF I'D KNOWN THE RIGHT TO VOTE WOULD MAKE WOMEN SO HORNY, I WOULD HAVE FOUGHT FOR THEIR EMANCIPATION CENTURIES EARLIER.

When those Fellowship of the Sun idiots started protesting outside our beloved bar, I felt a knot in my stomach. I imagine it's similar to what humans call gas pains, but I wouldn't know, since I'm not human. And even when I was human, briefly, I simply chose not to pass wind. I know you had your run-in with these Jesus freaks, but I couldn't quite grasp how irritating the religious right could be until they parked their pasty, chunky asses right outside our door.

The first few nights, I tried to ignore them. To pretend they weren't there. But where's the fun in that? So I started pickpocketing the bible thumpers in search of answers. The first few finds were as boring as they were to be expected: a pocket bible. Chapstick. Folded up fortunes from Chinese take out. Stale granola bars. Then I discovered this gem. A diamond in the rough, really:

Steve. Fucking. Newlin's *journal.*

Turns out the moron I swiped it from is not only a Fellowship of the Sun member, but also a law enforcement officer. And he just so happened to be the Deputy who found Steve Newlin's abandoned car on the side of Route 43 last January. Apparently Steve left a pray-in in search of some chicken and waffles and was never to be seen human again. This Dallas Deputy, a devout follower of the reverend, decided not to hand this over to evidence. What he was planning to do with it? Who the fuck knows. Who the fuck cares. All that matters is that it's in our hands now. It's not exactly a "dear diary" kind of book, but it's just as riveting. He calls it his "Field Guide." It's his homemade manual on vampires and other supes. You wouldn't believe the shit he's got in here. I read it twice, if I had bodily functions, I probably would have pissed myself laughing both times through. I couldn't resist adding some commentary.

You're welcome,

Pam

EELING
LPLESS?

THEN GET OUT THERE AND BE

HELPFUL!

JOIN US FOR A

PROTEST OUTSIDE SATAN'S DEN

(BETTER KNOWN AS "FANGTASIA," A VAMPIRE BAR IN SHREVEPORT).
444 INDUSTRIAL DRIVE, SHREVEPORT, LA

WE'LL GATHER FOR SIGN-PAINTING AT 4PM.
POSTERBOARD AND PAINTS WILL BE PROVIDED.**

PROTEST STARTS AT SUNSET.

My Dear Steve,

We live in exciting times. Since the "Great Revelation", our church has evolved and gained more followers in two years than in the past two decades. The message is loud and clear: Satan may have assembled an army, but God's army is bigger, stronger, and growing every single day.

However, this call to arms has alerted the enemy as well. The legions of the Great Beast have closed in on our family and staff. Nan Flanagan calls me a hatemonger on national television, and the Dallas vampire faction has sent me many thinly veiled threats "encouraging" me to cut back on my vitriol. I believe I am being followed. Perhaps I am being watched, even now, as I write this. I fear my days are numbered.

If you are reading this letter, then my suspicions have proven accurate and I am dead, felled at the hands of the dark minions of Satan. My assassination, like that of Archduke Ferdinand, whose death launched the first World War, is the first shot fired in the greatest battle of all: Armageddon.

Now that I am gone, it is your responsibility to become the man you were meant to be and lead our followers in my absence. You are a general in God's army now, Steve, and I know you understand this does not come without its dangers. It is not only your duty to protect humanity from Satan's wrath, but the lives of your stepmother, Yvette, and your baby sister, Bethany, as well. The vampires will stop at nothing to see the Newlin name wiped from the pages of history. I know you and Yvette have had your differences, but I must remind you that you are older than her, so please, treat her with the superior wisdom and patience I know you are capable of. I've seen you take loving command with Sarah and I ask you now to do the same with my wife and your sister. If they have survived my death, they will look to you for guidance now.

Do not grieve for me. Remember that every sunset is also a promise of a rising sun. God reminds us every day that though the darkness of night is inevitable, so is the glorious return of His light each and every morning. Rise up, my Son, and take your place at His side.

Praise His Light.

Your Loving Father,

Theodore Newlin

Theodore Newlin

SEPTEMBER 3RD

My father was a powerful force in my life. He was the strongest man I ever knew. I spent my Sundays as a child staring up at him from our congregation as he pounded his fist upon the lectern, filled with the fury of the Lord, until often his noble, bald head turned bright purple and he would collapse upon the cistern, breaking into wild convulsions brought on by the possession of the Holy Spirit. A feat made only more glorious when projected through the Jumbotron in our stadium-sized church arena. It made for great ratings.

In fact, for the first few years of my life, I thought that my father WAS God. Literally. After all, had I not seen him make the sick leap to their feet, tossing their wheelchairs and crutches into the crowd like the discarded wrappers of the multitude of fast food hamburgers that crippled them with diabetes and obesity? Had he not eradicated the sins from the weak with the touch of a hand so powerful it sent them flying into the air like the ejaculated souls of the damned from their graves on Judgment Day? The Bible teaches us that God performs miracles. And miracle making was my Daddy's bread and butter. He made it look easy, too.

The belief that I was the Son of God lasted until I was six years old, when my mother died from cervical cancer. I begged and pleaded for my father to save her, bring her back to life and restore her to the once radiant beauty that had been slowly drained of her, like blood from the neck of some lowly fangbanger. But he proved to be out of miracles that day. He wasn't God, he was just a man. But his strength, his commitment, his fury . . . that was given to him by our Heavenly father, and it's what shaped me into the man I am today.

LOWLY FANGBANGERS ARE BEST CHUGGED IN FIFTEEN SECONDS OR LESS.

It is my father's example that I cling to now, in my darkest hour. In the aftermath of what I refer to as "The Incident" at the Fellowship of the Sun, involving the raid by the Dallas vampires (my father's murderers), that she-bitch from Bon Temps, Sookie Stackhouse, and her vampire sex slaves, Eric Northman and Bill Compton, I have taken time to reflect upon my own strengths and weaknesses.

I see my defeat as a wake-up call from God. I didn't know that Godric had a progeny that would come to his rescue. I didn't know that Jason Stackhouse was a spy sent to infiltrate my camp. I didn't know that my wife Sarah was a harlot (although I should have seen that one coming - some of the things she wore to bed sent shivers up my spine, and not in a good way!). And you know why? I was spending too much time focusing on avenging my father's death, I was too distracted to see the real dangers surrounding me. The fact that I got out of there alive is a miracle, maybe one last trick performed by Daddy as he watched from above.

At any rate, I survived. And it appears that God still has a plan for me. I may have lost the battle, but the war is yet to be won.

While I navigate divorce and financial woes, and combat a new wave of evil on the airwaves (this Russell Edgington character is at the top of my list of vamps I'd like to penetrate with a stake!), I have also secretly gathered information on not just vampires and human-sympathizers like the Stackhouses, but other-yes OTHER-supernatural creatures enlisted in Satan's army! In fact, I have discovered that Bon Temps, hometown to that sex-addicted, mind-reading waitress, is itself a haven for Satan's legions. A real stomping ground for an entire host of demons and freaks. What I have learned will shock the world, but they didn't name the book "Revelations" for nothing!

Soon, I will reveal my discoveries to the world in what I call PHASE 2 of the Fellowship movement. I was caught unawares once. And like my hero George W. Bush said, "Fool me once, shame on you. Fool me -- you can't get fooled again." What follows is an instructional guide on how to detect, understand, and kill the creatures of Satan.

I'll make Daddy proud yet. When he finally returns to earth, commanding a host of heavenly warriors during the Final Battle with Satan himself, I'll be there, flaming sword in hand, to greet him with open arms, a ~~smiling face~~, and awe in my heart.

Now, TIME TO GO STAKE SOME FANGERS!!!

STAKING FANGERS IS A FAIRLY MESSY BUSINESS, STEVE, I'D HATE TO SEE YOUR PRETTY WHITE SUIT TURN RED.

LIGHT OF DAY
INSTITUTE
Fellowship
of the
SUN
"SEE YOU ON SUNDAY!"
EV. STEVE NEWLIN
wship of the Sun

VAMPIRES

~~A.K.A.~~ Vampers, Fangers, Leeches, Nightwalkers, the Undead

HUMANS

A.K.A. Bloodbags, Breathers, Meat Sacks, Organ Donors

MY OWN HISTORY WITH VAMPIRES

It seems to me that whenever I'm in a social setting -- a church BBQ, dinner with friends, poker night with the guys (we play with yogurt covered raisins instead of money, because we all know the Lord doesn't condone gambling!) -- the same set of questions arise: Where were you when vampires came out of the coffin? How did you find out? Did you know anyone that turned out to be a vampire?

Everyone has their story. They guard it like a Glenn Beck autograph, handling it with the utmost care but at the same time, brazenly telling all whenever they get the chance. I can only speak for myself, of course. I was gathered around the television in the Church's basement with my family. Everyone was there -- Daddy, his wife Yvette, my baby sister Bethany, Sarah, Sarah's parents, even Sarah's sister, Dot. We were drinking hot chocolate (with marshmallows!) and nibbling on Dot's homemade graham crackers while the news proved my father's worst fears to be true: Vampires walked amongst us. Pretty soon after it was announced, Daddy's publicist Leslie came in to whisk him off to go on the air and preach for humanity. And preach, he did. They put him on nearly every channel, both liberal and conservative, and boy, did he shine! It was his defining moment, I'd say. He told the world who he was and what he stood for, and well, the world listened. We must have sat there through the whole night, because by the time we switched off the television and climbed up the basement stairs, light was pouring through the stained glass windows like a big, warm hug from God Himself. It was a hug full of assurance, safety, and most importantly, hope.

Is THAT how you got so soft?

Yeah, that light really bounced off his FAT, BALD head

Everyone's been affected by vampires in some way. Whether directly or through someone you know or what you've read in the papers. There's no escaping it. I wish I could say otherwise, but I know all about it firsthand. Vampires killed my Daddy. According to the police report, he, Yvette and Bethany died in a "freak" car accident. They were on the highway when a sign on the overpass came crashing down in front of Daddy's Lincoln, and they smashed right into the debris, headfirst. The impact shattered his skull, and he peacefully floated up to the Heavens. Yvette's neck broke and she bled out, and Bethany, tiny thing that she was, died of a blunt trauma to the chest. But since I knew vampires have the ability to cover their tracks and make brutal killings look like unfortunate but natural occurrences, I never believed that report. Not for a blessed moment. Road signs of that size don't just randomly collapse when there's no wind in sight. I knew someone MADE that sign fall exactly where it did. Someone with fangs and a cold, dead heart. My suspicions were later confirmed by Texas Stan, who owned up to the "accident" like it was some proud victory, which only fueled the fire for me.

And consuming enough aerosol spray to hold up the Golden Gate Bridge

I find comfort in knowing that they're with God now, but I also have what Sarah used to call survivor's guilt. See, I was supposed to be with them that tragic night, but I made a last-minute decision to stay home. Sarah had recently been put on bed rest. Our doctor thought she was with child at the time. (Sadly we later learned it was one of those hysterical pregnancies.*) She urged me to go out and have fun with the fam, but it didn't seem very gentlemanly to leave her alone in that big old bed. I ordered some Hawaiian pizzas and cracked open a new puzzle, and we lay together thinking of baby names while slowly solving the jigsaw. We had just about settled on Barnabas Teddy Newlin when the phone rang.

Even though I'm happy to be here, to be writing these words and living what I preach on a daily basis, I can't help but ask myself why I wasn't in that car. Why I picked that night, of all nights, to stay home with my falsely pregnant wife. And the only sensible conclusion I've come to thus far is that it was all part of God's plan. That He spared me so I could continue Daddy's mission and make the world a better place for all God's creatures.

*I CAN'T HELP BUT ASK MYSELF THE **SAME QUESTION.***

* This was rather shocking to both of us, since we weren't even trying at the time! We hadn't been particularly active in the bedroom in quite a while, and even when we were, Sarah insisted we use the ever-reliant "pulling out" method. The doctor later said it may have been brought on by the stress of Sarah's post-wedding depression, which had been lingering for about four years.

Obituaries

Theodore Newlin dies at 51

Founder of the Fellowship of the Sun church and loving father of two

The son of Arkansas tobacco farmers Edna and George Newlin, Theodore Newlin, a preacher and popular televangelist, has died. He was 51. Newlin was killed yesterday in a horrific car accident on highway 10, alongside his daughter and wife. Powerful winds blew over an exit sign, which subsequently tumbled in his car's path. He was pronounced dead at the scene of the accident. He is survived only by his son, Reverend Steven Newlin. The time and place of the funeral will be announced on the fellowship's website Tuesday morning. The family is requesting privacy in this time of grief.

THE BROTHERHOOD OF THE ETERNAL SUN

Shortly after the Great Revelation, my father changed the name of our church from The First Dallas Fellowship of Man to the Fellowship of the Sun. The name seems like a natural fit for a pro-human/anti-vampire congregation, but few people know that the origins of the name, and our mission, can be traced back to medieval times and The Holy Christian Order of the Brotherhood of the Eternal Sun.

The Brotherhood of the Eternal Sun was an order of knights that spent most of the Middle Ages roaming the British countryside and parts of the European continent on a crusade against "daemons," or what we now know to be vampires. One will find little mention of the Brotherhood in history books and surviving legends of their quests have been regarded as just that: legend.

ACTUALLY THEY HAD LOTS OF STUPID NAMES FOR US, LIKE EKIMMU, OBOUR AND SKOFFIN. I'M GLAD WE'VE ALL SETTLED ON **VAMPIRE.**

In his book, Knights of the Dawn (Chronicle Books, 2009) vampire historian Josef Hinter describes the knights as having "a less popular reputation than their predecessors, The Knights Templar, but their legacy is essential in bringing the secret history of vampires into light." According to Hinter, the Brotherhood rose from the ashes of the Templar Knights, who were killed off by a faction of vampires that had infiltrated Pope Clément's inner circle (I tend to agree with this take on history; I've always said, never trust a Catholic). The Brotherhood, clad in SILVER ARMOR, swore revenge against these monsters and took an oath to hunt down this "blood drinking menagerie of Lucifer" and "slaye their daemonic kinde with staykes through theyre hearts." Although they did not use the term, "vampire," there can be no doubt that's exactly what these heroes were hunting.

I've always said NEVER trust a man who uses more hairspray than I do, Steve.

The Brotherhood of the Eternal Sun survived the Middle Ages and into the 16th century. Alas, their numbers dwindled, having been picked off over time

I KNEW JOSEF'S GREAT, GREAT GRANDFATHER RUDOLPH, WHO FANCIED HIMSELF A VAMPIRE HUNTER. HE WOULD BE ASHAMED TO KNOW THAT HIS DESCENDANTS WERE WRITING ABOUT VAMPIRES INSTEAD OF SLAYING THEM. AS FOR RUDY, LET'S JUST SAY THE MEAT ON HIS BONES WAS A LOT TOUGHER THAN HE WAS.

by an ever-increasing vampire population, and they were finally slain at the hand of Queen Mary I, or "Bloody Mary," who, according to Hinter, was turned vampire to save her from illness and subsequently crowned the Vampire Queen of England.* After the Brotherhood's extermination, vampires worked hard to ensure that the role the holy order played in history was suppressed.

However, God's work does not go unrewarded and some tales of the Brotherhood survived, even if a vampire-ignorant public regarded them as myth. My father first heard the legends of the Brotherhood when he was in his twenties and inducted to the local chapter of the Grand Architects, a club composed of the distinguished pillars of the Dallas community. During his initiation ceremony, Daddy was shown the gleaming, silver helm of a dead Brotherhood Knight that the Grand Architects safe-harbored as a symbol to overcome all types of injustices and evil. Daddy even said that the knight's helmet "whispered the secrets of God's plan into his ears," but he had been known to dip a little too far into the whiskey sometimes, and I know from experience that most of those boys were just a bunch of rowdy, rich cowboys. Whether or not his fellow fraternizers actually believed the tales of the so-called "Silver Knights," I'll never know, but their tales got my father hooked, and he would often regale me of their adventures while bouncing me on his knee by the fire when I was a boy. So it's no surprise when he later renamed our church in their honor and led his own modern-day crusade against fangers.

In addition to their silver armor, white or sometimes blue robes emblazoned with the sigil of a burning yellow sun could identify a member of the Brotherhood of the Eternal Sun. I must admit that I myself have borrowed those colors from time to time. If it ain't broke, don't fix it!

Because nothing says hardboiled killer quite like light blue and pale yellow.

* There seems to be some confusion around the true identity of this "Bloody Mary." In his first book, Decrypting Vampires, Hinter originally supposes it was Mary Stuart -- not Mary Tudor -- who inherited the nickname from her cousin after her turning. He later recants this mistake in Knights of the Dawn while interviewing a surviving member of Bloody Mary's underground court, who goes on to insist Mary Stuart could not have turned after her beheading. She was in fact Queen Mary Tudor I, older sister of Queen Elizabeth Tudor I. The identity of this vampire informant remains anonymous and sadly, was not slain by Hinter.

Eric has one of these suits of armor in his collection of meaningless shit in the basement.

MEANINGLESS SHIT IS A LITTLE HARSH, PAM, CONSIDERING THIS SUIT SAVED YOUR LIFE ONCE. NOT TO MENTION THE TROUBLE I WENT THROUGH TO GET IT. I WAS TRAVELING THROUGH THE FOREST OF BORCÉLIANDE WHEN I MET SIR JUSTAIN BUBARÉ AND MANAGED TO DISARM HIM USING ONLY ONE LEATHER GLOVE AND A PAIR OF FANGS.

IS THERE A VAMPIRE BIBLE?

There are all sorts of "bibles" out there. The Torah, the Koran, the Ethiopic Bible (which boasts a lengthy 81 books-it's a doozy), and the real bible, the divinely inspired one, the Holy Bible.

I was a fairly studious kid growing up, so when I became a Reverend I thought I knew all there was to know about different religious texts . . . until Daddy told me about the possible existence of a "Vampire Bible." It was only a short while after the Great Revelation, and Daddy had been hard at work mobilizing the Fellowship of the Sun. After a long day of recruiting at a prison outside Dallas with our faithful friend and follower, Orry Dawson, Daddy sat me down, poured me a whiskey and told me a story that shook me to my very core.

An Episcopal bishop, Victor Clayton Vlazny III, with whom my father did missionary work in Estonia, had contacted Daddy earlier that day. Vlazny claimed he had confronted a vampire cult that had taken residence in an abandoned house in a bad part of town that apparently worshipped the demon Lilith. Surprised and outraged to discover a human witnessing their strange ritual, the beasts attacked the poor clergyman. The bishop only managed to escape the hideous creatures by waving a silver cross in their direction (at the time we still weren't sure if it was the silver or the cross that had fended off his attackers). Vlazny went on to describe what he witnessed as "a strange blood drinking ceremony where the vampires read from a bastardized version of the Bible while paying homage to the Mother of Vampires." To make matters more alarming, Vlazny went missing days later. He's never been heard from since.

Could there be a vampire religion that worships this Lilith character, complete with its own sacrilegious texts? I suppose anything is possible at this point, but ~~I have a hard time~~ believing that vampires worship anything other than their own vanity.

I DO LOVE IT WHEN THEY KNEEL BEFORE ME.

However, the name Lilith rang a bell, taking me back to my late night cram sessions back in seminary. There is some debate in the Church around the existence of Lilith. The word lilit appears in some translations of the Book of Isaiah, in reference to a demonic, dirty animal. The name "Lilith" shows up in the Dead Sea Scrolls, listed alongside other wicked creatures. In other texts, mostly regarded as heretical, Lilith was Adam's first wife, or his estranged, evil twin that slept with Satan and gave birth to the first "djinn" (i.e. vampire). This is why she is known in some stories as the "the mother of demons." I

I don't need to worship my God-given assets. I have clientele that do that for me.

think with the emergence of vampires, the legend of Lilith deserves closer examination. Who knows, perhaps she still walks amongst us today?

Whether or not a "vampire bible," exists, the world may never know. But it does make sense that a religion ran by a woman would involve a lot of blood sucking. UNFORTUNATELY, THE BOOK OF VAMPYR IS VERY REAL... AND A VERY REAL PAIN IN MY ASS.

SURVEILLANCE AND RECONNAISSANCE

My followers have often asked me, "Steve, how do you know so much about vampires?"

Well, a lot of what I know I picked up from Daddy. He was a much better scholar than I. In fact, he was working on a wonderful and informative book called Satan Revealed: How Vampires Took Over the World and How to Take It Back before he was assassinated. Many of his notes are compiled here and I may yet go back and finish the book myself.

I did have one advantage over my father, however. I had something Daddy never had in his possession: a real-life vampire! In the weeks I spent with Godric as my prisoner, I was able to obtain some vital information from him on the nature of their kind. Surprisingly-and I must admit somewhat disappointingly-this did not require any form of torture. Godric gave me this information willingly, almost amicably. When I asked him why he was so readily sharing the secrets of his race, he told me he'd made peace with the fact that he would soon be leaving this earth permanently, and wanted to do something good-for both human- and vampirekind-with his final nights. He thought that perhaps by opening up to me, I might see whatever traces of humanity he still had left, and instead of continuing my mission to eradicate vampires, I might forge a more peaceful path of coexistence. Did I believe a word he said? Of course not. His submission was merely a sign to me that vampires are God-fearing cowards at heart. This explains why they spent so many centuries hiding their existence from humanity. They know we have the power to destroy them.

GODRIC, AS A VAMPIRE, IS MORE **MAN** THAN YOU COULD EVER **DREAM** OF BEING.

On my quest to learn more about the enemy following "The Incident" at the church, I spent some time doing what any good soldier would do: a little reconnaissance. I followed Sookie Stackhouse back to Bon Temps and laid low for a time, spying on her during her adventures and gathering as much information about the supernatural world as possible. (I even witnessed what appeared to be one of the gosh-darned strangest weddings I'll ever see, involving a giant meat sculpture, human sacrifice, and a live bull. Not sure what to make of that whole thing-but it smacked of Satanic ritual!)

But I digress. The following is what I know to be true about vampirekind . . .

WHAT ARE VAMPIRES?

This is a question I've been trying to answer since Daddy first told me about them. Of course they're bloodsucking creatures of Satan, but what are they, physically speaking? They look like humans, only paler, colder to the touch. They've got skin and bones, fingernails, and hair. But they're not like us, this much we know. The only thing inside their casing is vampire blood, or "V." Ain't nothing else coursing through them. No veins, no muscles, no intestines or reproductive system. No bodily fluids or bodily functions, really. It's almost like biology doesn't apply to them! If they didn't come from the same planet, I might be inclined to call them aliens! I suppose the best way to boil it down is this: they're essentially reanimated corpses that drink our blood. Pleasant, isn't it?

HOW DOES A VAMPIRE "TURN" A HUMAN?

1. Vampire drains human victim of his blood.
2. Vampires replace victim's blood with his own vampire blood, also known as "V."
3. Vampire sleeps in the ground with victim's dead body during day.
4. Human rises from ground as vampire the next night.

HOW DO THEY SUBSIST?

Ever since the advent of the synthetic blood substitute, vampires and humans alike have been saying that vampires can survive on Tru Blood and Tru Blood alone. But putting your faith in that is like voting for a Democrat! Vampires eat humans, plain and simple. They suck the blood from our veins and when our veins have gone dry, they find another human to victimize. Tru Blood is a lie the liberal media tells the world to help people sleep better at night. True vampire nature desires-nay, demands!-human blood for subsistence. Without it, vampires go weak. They fade away as a starved human would, only slower and more gruesomely. It's unclear to me how much blood vampires need to live on; it seems to depend on how much energy they expend. But a well-fed vamp is about as strong as any supernatural creature can get.

MUCH TO MY OWN SURPRISE, VAMPIRES CAN SUBSIST ENTIRELY ON TRU BLOOD. I DISCOVERED THIS FIRSTHAND WHEN I WAS IN MINNESOTA AT A NORDIC VAMPIRE CONFERENCE, AND A FELLOW VIKING, MADS, DARED ME TO SWEAR OFF HUMAN BLOOD FOR A WEEK. IT WAS A CHILDISH BET, I'LL ADMIT, AND WHILE THEY WERE PASSING AROUND YOUNG BLONDE SCANDIES I WAS TEMPTED TO GIVE IN, BUT $10,000 IN GOLD WAS A MUCH BETTER PRIZE

VAMPIRE STRENGTHS

GLAMOURING: The method by which vampires hypnotize innocent humans into doing, thinking, or feeling whatever ungodly things they want us to.

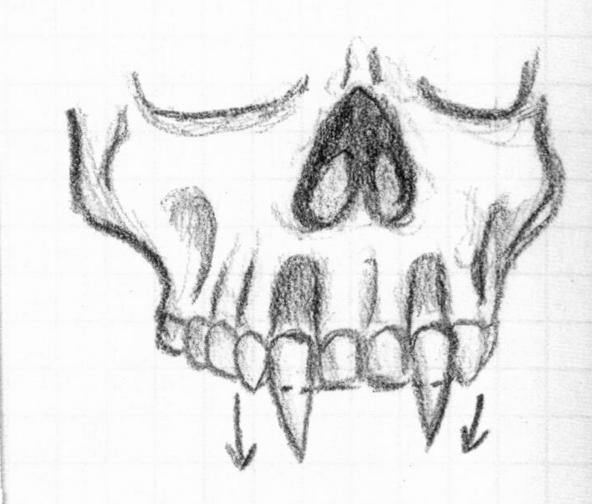

FANGS: Long, sharp teeth characteristic of all vampires. Much like a rattlesnake's fangs, a vampire's fangs recede into the roof of his mouth until they pop out for feeding. While newer vampires have trouble controlling their fangs, the actual length of the teeth increases with age and/or power. Vampires often display their fangs when hungry or sensing danger.

We call this a fang-out.

We call this a fang boner.

VAMP SPEED: The enhanced speed at which a vampire can move. This applies not only to running, but also to household chores. *—and text messaging*

ENHANCED SENSES: Vampires' auditory perception, vision, and olfaction is far superior to that of humans. It assists them in the detection of any potential surrounding dangers.

FLIGHT: Some vampires-but not all-possess the ability to fly. It is believed to be a skill makers can pass on to their progeny.

If only . . . This gene must have skipped a generation. Eric can fly and I'm stuck on the ground. It's really a shame; it would certainly make it a lot easier to get around in heels.

PHYSICAL STRENGTH: Vampires are unequivocally stronger than their human counterparts. Their muscles are even more powerful than those belonging to Jason Stackhouse. And he's pretty husky.

HEALING: When vampires suffer cuts, bruises, broken bones, or other injuries, they heal within moments, a serious advantage on the battlefield. We know this to be true, because we recently tested this theory on Godric while he was our prisoner. My assistant Gabe sliced his arm up like a watermelon on a summer's day, and by golly, the cuts mended within seconds!

VAMPIRE WEAKNESSES

HEP-D: A blood-borne virus that does not affect humans but can enervate vampires for weeks at a time. Whether or not it can kill vampires has yet to be ascertained.

If treated properly, Hep-D ain't gonna kill anyone. Except for maybe the human carrying it, because I don't know any vampire that would let them get away with it.

THE BLEEDS: When a vampire forces himself to stay awake during the day, he experiences a weakened state, the symptoms of which include bleeding out of the nose and ears. AND EYES His or her energy will slowly deplete until the vampire gets some rest.

SILVER: The metallic element (Ag) burns vampire skin and weakens a vampire's strength. The purer the silver, the more powerful the effects.

I'VE HEARD THAT RUSSELL EDGINGTON USED TO PUNISH VAMPIRE UNDERLINGS WITH COLLOIDAL SILVER ENEMAS. THAT IS TRULY SICK, BUT I HAVE TO GIVE HIM POINTS FOR CREATIVITY.

SUNLIGHT: Vampires cannot be exposed to the sun (or any UV rays for that matter, even if they're artificial), or they will burn to a crisp.

WELL, THERE IS A WAY . . .

FOOD: Human food stimulates nausea. Yes, I'd consider it a weakness never getting to enjoy Sarah's finger-licking-good ribs! Those baby-back delights are almost worth staying together for . . . Almost.

THRESHOLDS: Vampires cannot just enter a human's house; they have to be invited in. This does not apply to public buildings or vampires' homes.

OR YOU CAN JUST BUY THE HOUSE.

HEP-V: Still in early trial periods, this bio-agent poisons vampires by destroying their bodies from the inside out. It's much like its precursor HEP-D, but much faster and more effective. This may turn out to be a fantastic way to quietly exterminate the vampire species!

ULTIMATE WEAKNESS: The Lord. Jesus Hates Fangs.

MISCELLANEOUS OBSERVATIONS AND TERMINOLOGY

TURNING: The method in which a vampire transforms a human into his own Satan-loving kind (see previous).

When they cry, they cry tears of blood. Boo-frickin'-hoo.

Hair doesn't grow back.

Vampires don't use the toilet. Ever. Can't decide if this is a strength (time saved) or a weakness (I do some of my best thinking on the john).

They often form "nests," which leads to more aggressive, territorial behavior.

MOST PREFERRED FEEDING LOCATION: femoral artery.

Tell me, Steve, when was the last time you had your head between a woman's legs?

Two-thirds of new vampires do not survive the first year.

If a vampire is in a weakened state, he may have trouble releasing his ~~fangs~~. *We call this dropping fang.*

They typically bury dead humans in fresh graves to avoid detection.

Vampires are preserved exactly as they were the night they were turned. They'll be fifteen, fat, or acne-prone forever.

Or a virgin . . . poor Jessica.

TRUE DEATH: The term referring to a vampire's death.

VAMPIRE BLOOD AND ITS USES/ABUSES

I can't deny the fact that vampire blood has healing properties that can sometimes seem miraculous. But don't be fooled! This marvel comes at a price: destruction. Vampire blood is a highly addictive substance, creating mania in its users and destroying the lives of countless humans. Many begin taking it recreationally, and experience a "high" that involves hallucinations and enhanced strength. But soon, the body begins to crave more, and overuse can lead to some awful things, like priapism (ouchie zowchie!) and severe mental disturbances. I recently started a rehab program for recovering V addicts that has a 92 percent success rate! But I'll get into the details of that later.

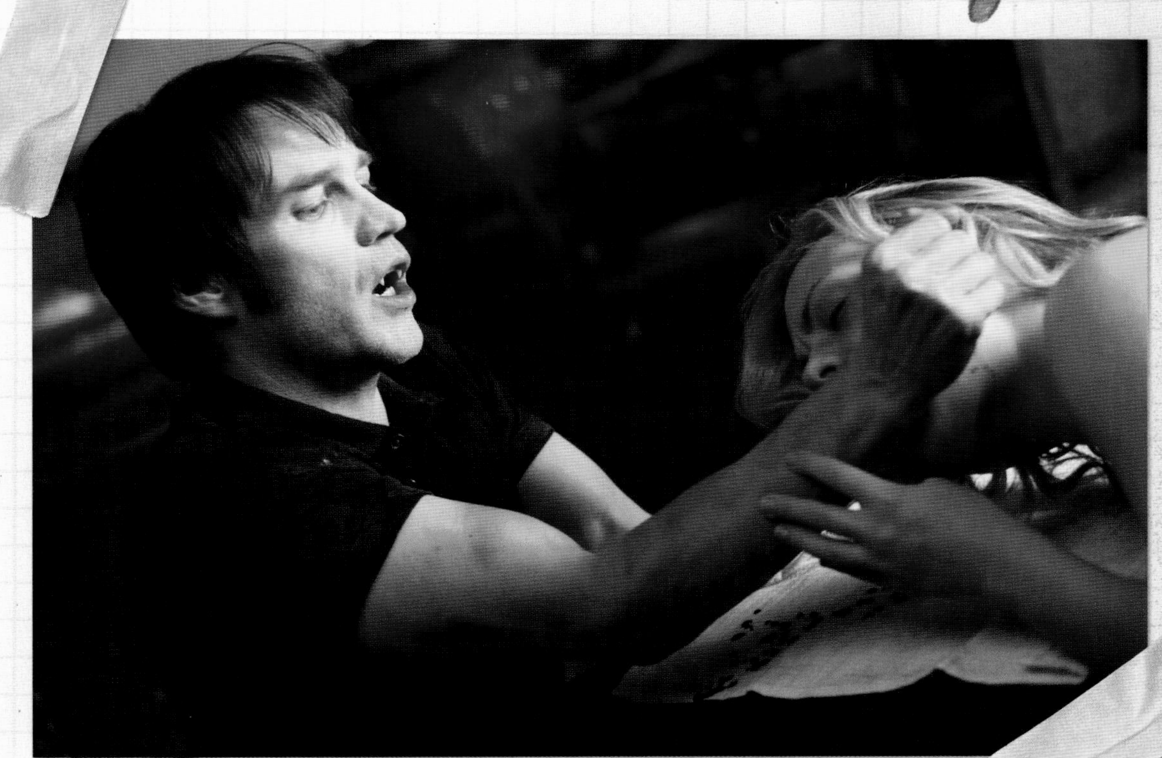

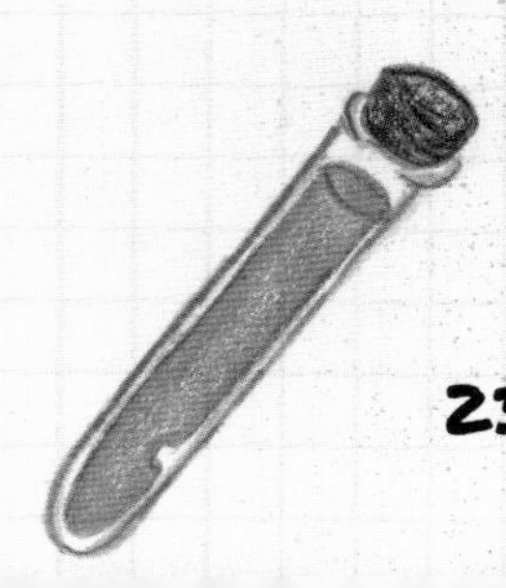

Because your traditional family unit did such a great job raising you? Haven't you read the latest studies? Gay couples and makers are the best parents out there.

BYLAWS OF THE MAKER/PROGENY RELATIONSHIP

Much like a little boy has his father, or a little girl her mother, baby vampires have makers. But in place of offering a pat on the back and a "go get 'em, champ," or a supple teat full of wholesome milk, makers foster the bloodlust of their progeny and teach them skills like killing and draining. It's worse than two men trying to raise a kid together! But I digress . . . Let's get back to the facts, shall we? The maker/progeny relationship comes with a set of rules and governing principles, some of them physical, and some of them historical, but all of them crucial to vampire constitution.

The Law of Obedience

As much of a pain in the ass being a maker has been, this is a definite perk.

When makers say "As your maker, I command you," their progeny must obey. Defiance is not an option.

The Law of Sexual Favors

Progeny act as sexual aides for their makers. They must always bow down to sexual requests, regardless of their absurdity.

Really, Steve? Not that I wouldn't bow down to any of Eric's sexual requests, he's a Viking god after all . . But there are no requirements in this arena. This bylaw is a big, fat piece of BS.

The Summoning Statute

Makers have the ability to summon or demand the presence of their progeny. The call sends shivers through the younger vampires, no matter how far apart they may be, and this feeling helps guide them in the direction of their makers.

Danger Sense

When makers or progeny find themselves in danger or in great pain, their counterparts will feel a vibration of fear indicating they are in trouble. This vibration can also guide vampires in the direction of their makers or progeny.

The Superiority Decree

Vampires can almost never overpower their makers. It is exceedingly rare and has only occurred a few times in history. (Godric, the vampire held in my captivity, managed to overthrow a maker he described as "wicked down to the bone.")

The Ordinance of Handshakes

All maker/progeny relationships maintain their very own secret handshake, which often acts as a pre-feeding ritual to prepare vampires for fresh blood.

Where in the world did Steve come up with this shit? Secret handshakes? What is this, a slumber party?

How To Kill a Vampire

an Illustrated Guide

text by
Sarah Newlin

800
CALL 555
PAT 0199

By stake:

Acquire a wooden stake, or make your own!

By fire:

Fire will also do the trick!

Step back and turn away!

WARNING: KILLING A VAMPIRE IS THE ONLY TIME IT'S OKAY TO PLAY WITH MATCHES!

By sunlight:

In the sun,
it's lots of fun!

Tie a vampire to a giant cross! Be sure to use silver chains!

Wait until sunrise and then let God finish the job!

Step back and turn away!

COMMON MISCONCEPTIONS

Sometimes, when it comes to vampires, it's hard to separate fact from fiction. The Internet, the papers, and countless news programs are flooded with misinformation, thanks to the liberal media. So I am thrilled to say that I've proven the following beliefs about vampires to be UNTRUE:

CROSSES CAN HARM OR TURN AWAY A VAMPIRE. I'm still wrapping my head around this one. We know vamps are creatures of Satan, so you would think a cross would at least make them blink, or send them a static shock. Perhaps fangers have shown such little regard for all that is holy over the centuries that they have become completely desensitized to Christian iconography?

HOLY WATER BURNS A VAMPIRE. Also a head-scratcher. I can come to no other conclusion than that holy water has become too polluted with sins over the years to have any overwhelming effect on evil.

The logic of fundamentalists never ceases to entertain me. Or shut down my lady parts.

MIRRORS DO NOT REFLECT VAMPIRES. This one is just Hollywood garbage. Everyone knows vampires are so vain they must spend half the night in front of mirrors, making sure they've got their leather buckled in all the right places.

GARLIC REPELS VAMPIRES. Completely false! At the most, it can act as a mild irritant to their heightened sense of smell, but vampires have no notable relationship with this species of onion. Although I do recommend consuming large portions of this for those nights when the missus is feeling frisky, but you just aren't in the mood. One whiff of your breath and you'll both be off to dreamland in no time flat!

ALL VAMPIRES ARE "SEXY." Although I do believe vampires seek more conventionally good-looking humans to victimize and turn, I've seen a few that could strip the paint off a pickup truck with one glance. And once an ugly vamp, always an ugly vamp.

VAMPIRES CAN SHAPE-SHIFT INTO BATS AND WOLVES.* These powers are reserved for other creatures of Satan. Read on into the depths of this Field Guide, and ye shall see . . .

* Bats are still the most frightening animals on the face of the earth. Even writing about them gives me the creepy-crawlies. One summer, I discovered a nest of bats had formed in the attic of our guesthouse. I sent Sarah out there armed with a hose and a can of insecticide while I watched from the safety of the kitchen windows. We ended up in the ER that night and she got two rabies shots in her stomach. I eventually gave in and burned the guesthouse to the ground.

I couldn't have been more proud of the Fellowship of the Sun when we captured Godric. He was the oldest vampire we'd encountered-which also means he was the strongest. Godric capitulated peacefully, which was a shock, really, but perhaps he knew he was destined to lose this species war. He was definitely smarter than most of the vampires I've met. Maybe brains comes with age too-not that vampires have brains. Anyway, you get the point. You'll find in the following pages a collection of KNOWN ENEMIES, vampires I've had the pleasure of capturing, spying on, or simply observing.

KNOWN ENEMY

NAME Godric

SPECIES Vampire

AGE Approximately 2,000 years old

STATUS Deceased

OCCUPATION Sheriff of Area 9 in Texas

MAKER Roman commander, name unknown

KNOWN PROGENY Eric Northman

AND MY DEAR SISTER NORA GAINSBOROUGH

NOTES

As far as physicality goes, he was short, with boyish looks, kind of like a teenager. When we interrogated him, he opened up about his past. Originally from Gaul, Godric was captured as a slave and turned by his Roman master. He hated his master with a fury, and eventually killed him, a rare feat in the vampire world. He expressed some sorrow and regret about his past, about the wars he'd once fought in and the humans he'd obliterated, which I'm sure was just a ploy to pull my heartstrings, hoping I'd take pity on his woes and set him free. But Daddy taught me better than that!

KNOWN ENEMY

NAME Eric Northman

SPECIES Vampire

AGE Approximately 1,000 years old

STATUS Active

OCCUPATION Sheriff of Area 5/local business owner

MAKER Godric

KNOWN PROGENY Pamela Swynford de Beaufort

How the fuck did he know my full name? Eric knew not to tell ANYONE. Must have been that stupid estate lawyer when Eric was drawing up his will . . .

NOTES

A Viking prince in his human life, Eric's name was originally spelled "Erik," Old Norse for "eternal ruler." Godric had witnessed the Viking's skill on the battlefield and, impressed with his prowess, decided to turn him. Eric was fatally wounded and had already suffered the slaughter of his entire family, so he welcomed the transformation as a gift. Eric became a maker himself in the early 1900s, when he turned brothel owner and part-time prostitute Pamela. In the wake of the Great Revelation, Eric sought to capitalize on humans' curiosity about vampires, and opened a vampire-themed bar called Fangtasia. He has also, on occasion, dabbled in the illegal sale of V. I captured this slickster once, with aims to introduce him to the sun, but Sookie Stackhouse and Godric freed him during "The Incident" at the Fellowship of the Sun lock-in. If I caught him once, I can catch him again!

KNOWN ENEMY

NAME William B. Compton

SPECIES Vampire

AGE Approximately 174 years old

STATUS Active

OCCUPATION King of Louisiana

MAKER Lorena Krasiki

KNOWN PROGENY Jessica Hamby

NOTES

Originally from Bon Temps, Bill left his human family behind to serve as First Lieutenant in the 28th Louisiana Infantry during the Civil War. On his journey home after the Confederates surrendered, Bill encountered his maker, Lorena Krasiki, and was never to return to his wife, Caroline, and children, Thomas and Sarah, as a man again. Despite a tombstone in the Bon Temps cemetery that reads BELOVED HUSBAND, FATHER, BRAVE SOLDIER, Bill decided to return to his roots and settle down in Bon Temps after the Great Revelation. After the mysterious death of Queen Sophie-Anne, Bill was crowned king of Louisiana, and appears to have ties to Nan Flanagan and her shadow government. He's particularly strong and savvy for his age, his only weakness a soft spot for Sookie Stackhouse. There must be something about that girl.

Her magic faerie "portal," you mean?

KNOWN ENEMY

NAME Jessica Hamby

SPECIES Vampire

AGE Only 17 when turned, Hamby is still considered a "baby vamp"

STATUS Active

OCCUPATION Merlotte's hostess

MAKER Bill Compton

KNOWN PROGENY None

NOTES

Jessica was raised in a loving, nuclear, God-fearing family before she was ripped from her peaceful adolescence and made vampire as part of Bill Compton's sentencing for killing vampire Longshadow, Fangtasia's delinquent bartender. She has since used her sanguine nature to corrupt humanity, seducing God-fearing Christian Hoyt Fortenberry, into a torrid love affair. When home alone, Jessica blasts pop music-she's particularly fond of Taylor Swift-and dances around her quarters in her skivvies.

REMEMBER WHEN YVETTA WAS SO PISSED THAT SHE WASN'T IN MY WILL AND RAN OUT ON US? WHAT SHE DIDN'T KNOW IS THAT SHE WAS IN MY WILL. I WAS BEQUEATHING HER TO YOU.

KNOWN ENEMY

NAME Pamela Swynford de Beaufort

SPECIES Vampire

AGE ~~Approximately 107 years old~~ I haven't aged a minute past 34

STATUS Active

OCCUPATION Fangtasia manager

Manager? Please. I'm so much more than that . . . I prefer the title Chief Creative Officer.

MAKER Eric Northman

KNOWN PROGENY None

First that disaster Colin, and now Tara fucking Thornton. At least she's got a great ass and a thing for ladies.

NOTES

~~The dearly beloved progeny of Eric Northman, Pamela is the sole heir to all of his properties and holdings.~~ She handles most of the business at Fangtasia, managing the vampire bar's day-to-day needs, whether it involves working the front door or cooking the books. Originally from England, Pamela was sent away by her conservative parents for engaging in explicit acts with many of the potential suitors they brought her. She found herself alone and broke in San Francisco, where she started working her way up the streets until eventually founding her very own whorehouse. It was there that she met Eric Northman, in California on vampire business, and left behind her human life. She has since preferred to lead a homosexual lifestyle, only fanning the flames of the fire in her future home: hell.

Nobody calls it a "lifestyle" anymore, Steve. Call me queer or better yet, don't call me at all.

And FYI, hell is "hot" for a reason.

KNOWN ENEMY

NAME Stan Baker, aka "Texas Stan"

SPECIES Vampire

AGE Approximately 300 years old

STATUS Deceased

OCCUPATION Former King of Texas/Terrorist

MAKER Unknown

KNOWN PROGENY None

As far as I'm concerned, his biggest crime was trying to pull off that cowboy hat.

NOTES

Stan is one of those rare breeds who sought out life as a vampire for the simple joy of being more powerful than the humans around him. His moral character is as shallow as the kiddie pool at my country club. A pioneer in the late 18th century, Stan went on to be a scout in the Civil War and eventually a trail and hunting guide for British royalty. He fancied himself a true American cowboy, and even appeared in his own TV show in the late 1950s called Texas Stan's Scouts on the Prairie. Beneath his vanity, he was a vicious vampire who abused his power to terrorize the Fellowship of the Sun. He brutally murdered my father, Yvette, and Bethany, and met his fate when brave Soldier of the Sun, Luke McDonald, set off a bomb in Godric's lair. May Stan rest in the bowels of hell forever. Amen.

LAST I HEARD, ISABEL TURNED DOWN
THE POSITION OF SHERIFF OF AREA 9
AND MENDED FENCES WITH MR. AYRES.
THEY NOW LIVE TOGETHER IN BENNINGTON,
VERMONT, WHERE THEY OWN A BED-AND-BREAKFAST.

KNOWN ENEMY

NAME Isabel

SPECIES Vampire

AGE Approximately 457 years old

STATUS Active

OCCUPATION AVL employee/terrorist

MAKER Unknown

KNOWN PROGENY None

NOTES

Born in Spain in 1551, Isabel de Castille was a descendent of royalty. The great granddaughter of Queen Isabel, she was married off at a young age in an effort to secure political alliances. Unhappy with her situation, Isabel asked her French vampire lover to turn her. In more recent years, she lived with her human companion Hugo Ayres, a lawyer who had been doing pro bono work for the AVL before coming to his senses and joining our forces. Despite his pleas to be made vampire so they could live together forever, Isabel refused-perhaps the only decent thing she's ever done. She worked tirelessly with Stan and other vampires in their nest to take down my church and all we stand for. She managed to escape Luke's attack unscathed, and rumor has it, she may have replaced Godric as Sheriff of Area 9, but I've yet to see her resurface.

KNOWN ENEMY

NAME Lorena Krasiki

SPECIES Vampire

AGE Approximately 252 years old

STATUS Deceased

OCCUPATION Unemployed

MAKER Istvan (last name unknown)

KNOWN PROGENY Mary Rieser, Bill Compton

NOTES

Born out of wedlock in 1759, Lorena was raised by a convent of nuns in Vienna. Just when she was about to take her vows and become a nun herself, a particularly evil vampire named Istvan turned the bastard child. Lorena adopted his wicked ways and engaged in the torture and murder of countless humans. Once an ally of the vampire king of Mississippi, Russell Edgington, she was eventually staked and killed by Sookie Stackhouse.

Including some of my best girls. She was one of the worst vampires to pass through my brothel. I like to call it hate at first sight.

KNOWN ENEMY

NAME Chow Lin

SPECIES Vampire

AGE Approximately 150 years old

STATUS Deceased

OCCUPATION Bartender and "fixer"

MAKER Unknown

KNOWN PROGENY None

NOTES

Born and raised in rural China, Chow led a quiet life as a carpenter. Upon witnessing a bloodthirsty vampire about to attack the woman he had loved from afar for 10 years (Chow suffered from crippling shyness), Chow offered his own life in place of hers. Despite this gesture, the woman never did return Chow's affections. When Bill staked Longshadow, Eric and Pamela employed Chow to take over his duties as part-time bartender and "fixer" of problems at Fangtasia. He took a somewhat lengthy leave of absence, departing Bon Temps on personal business, and returned to his post with a new look: a shaved head and fake goatee. Unfortunately for Chow, he was not very good at his job, as he was slain by a rebellious vampire named Remus and wound up in a box of Chinese takeout. Ironic, isn't it?

KNOWN ENEMY

NAME Russell Edgington (formerly known by his Celtic birth name "Korun")

SPECIES Vampire

AGE Approximately 3,000 years old

STATUS Unknown

OUT OF THE GROUND AND IN YOUR ARMS, STEVE. I'VE NEVER SEEN YOU LOOK SO HAPPY.

OCCUPATION King of Mississippi

MAKER Unknown

KNOWN PROGENY Talbot

NOTES

Russell Edgington and I have two things in common: we both were opposed to the Great Revelation (for different reasons, obviously) and we both have fantastic hair. Perhaps the oldest and most powerful vampire to walk the earth, Russell Edgington is also the most famous. He made himself a household name when he ripped out the spine of news anchor Jerry McCafferty on live television. While I can't condone this kind of action, Jerry was a registered Democrat, so maybe this was God's way of telling us it was time for him to go. Born before the birth of Christ himself, much of Russell's past is unknown. He's a mysterious sort, who uses werewolves to handle his dirty work, and after a brief disappearance post-World War II, he re-emerged as the vampire king of Mississippi. He had been living in sin with his progeny and lover for almost 700 years, until Talbot met the sharp end of a stake at the hand of Eric Northman.

REVENGE IS BEST SERVED NAKED ON A BEARSKIN RUG.

I'M HOLDING OFF ON THE FINAL COURSE WITH RUSSELL DURING MY TIME HERE IN THE AUTHORITY. BUT ONE MISSTEP FROM THAT SLICK-TALKING NAZI AND HE'LL END UP ON THE WRONG END OF MY STAKE. AND NOT THE ONE I GAVE TALBOT.

KNOWN ENEMY

NAME Sarah Newlin

SPECIES Human

AGE 32 (even though she tells everyone she's 29)

STATUS Unknown

OCCUPATION ~~Cheating, lying, traitorous whore~~ Ex-wife/romance novelist/ slanderer

MAKER

KNOWN PROGENY

NOTES

She may not be a real vamp, but she'll suck you dry, that's for sure, Steve.

Yeah, everyone but you, Steve.

September 17

You know, maybe I was a little hard on my soon-to-be ex wife during that last Field Guide entry. I don't usually like to "let the beast out," as I sometimes refer to that deep, caged anger inside of us all.

During my tenure as a reverend, I haven't been just a vampire hunter–I've been a healer of hearts. I've counseled many different couples on how to turn their marriages around, and I've found that when conversation has failed, it's sometimes best to write your feelings down. Maybe I should take my own advice and vent a little on what's been going on in my own marriage, if I can even call it that now.

Obviously, I was upset when Jason confessed he'd slept with my wife. I'm still working through it . . . It's been confusing, emotionally, to say the least. I know God is trying to teach me something here, but I can't see the lesson. It's weird because I almost feel less angry about the infidelity, and more upset that I was left out of the proceedings . . . At any rate, that's not the important issue.

The fact is, after "The Incident" at the church, SARAH decided she wanted to leave our marriage, not I, and promptly after announcing our separation, she signed a book deal and cranked out (in a matter of days, I might add!) a trashy, borderline pornographic romance novella called Sunset. And she's using the Newlin name to sell it!

The characters are all "fictional," but I can see the thinly-veiled caricatures for who they really are. The hackneyed story tells of a demure, Christian Southern belle named "Sandra Bowery," who falls in love with a sexy, strapping vampire slayer named "Jackson Stakehold." The handsome and muscle-bound Stakehold rescues Sandra from a sad marriage to her wicked husband, Stanley, and they run off to hunt down (and at one point, even engage in SEXUAL RELATIONS WITH) a cadre of vampires. And the kicker? In the end, Stanley returns as a vampire, and Sarah, I mean "Sandra," stakes him!

Pure smut.

This is all an attempt on Sarah's part to destroy my brand. My lawyers have been pursuing legal action, but until the divorce papers are filed, I've been told Sarah can use the Newlin name to sell anything she wants. Well, I'm certainly not going to cave. I may not be wearing my wedding band, but I'll be dead before I file. When Daddy split from his second wife, Charity, after her sordid past as an exotic dancer came to the media's attention, he said that when it came to ending a marriage, "The first to file is the first to flame," which was a reference to burning in hell. I admit, it wasn't his catchiest proverb, but he was right. And besides, seeking divorce is a sign of weakness and we all know that I am far stronger than Sarah.

I have to say, God is really testing my character. I just found out that Sarah is already fast at work on a new book, this one being a tell-all called Sundressed: The Sarah Newlin Story. Well folks, the title says it all.

The 10:00 A.M. contemporary service was over. The congregation had retreated to their homes and the pastor had retired to his office. They were alone at the altar. Alone at last, thought Sandra. She had been waiting for this moment since the day she first laid eyes on Jackson Stakehold. She could never forget the scent of his sweat and the glow of his skin beneath his sheer white tank top. He was the most beautiful specimen she had ever encountered. It shook her to the core, really, because she had never before imagined herself bedding a man besides the one she had perhaps too hastily married on her nineteenth birthday. How could she know what else would be out there to feast on at such a young age?

Sandra was quickly thrown out of her reverie by the sight of Jackson's chest. It was hairless, smooth, and tight. Exactly as she had pictured it so many times before. With his shirt now at his feet, Jackson Stakehold slowly unzipped his ever-tightening jeans, finally releasing his bulging manhood. Sandra could not believe this was actually happening. She had dreamt about it night after night, and never believed God would answer her prayers. Sandra clutched her throbbing breast with fear and pleasure as she gasped, "I've never done it in a church before!"

I hate to admit it, but this bitch can write.

THE GREAT REVELATION AND THE ADVENT OF TRU BLOOD

The Great Revelation is a term that's a little hard for me to stomach, because it borrows its title from the Revelation of John in the closing chapter of the Bible to describe the fateful night when vampires "came out of the coffin." Though, I must admit, as much I dislike the name, it is fitting for an event that essentially kicked off the apocalypse, so I suppose I'll "let it roll," as our youth group often says.

The Great Revelation, as I have said before, was one of, if not the most, significant moments in human history. It was essentially the equivalent of watching little green men land on the lawn of the White House and high-five the president. The human race found out that we were not alone.

Now THATS something I'd like to see.

TRU BLOOD -- A synthetic blood substitute that claims to sustain vampires. Like regular blood, Tru Blood has a limited shelf life. It is considered to be an acquired taste, perhaps similar to meal replacement shakes that my hefty Aunt Shirley used to drink.

Of course, any GFC (God-Fearing Christian) understands that the devil has been working behind the scenes to manipulate mankind's journey on God's green earth since the serpent got Eve to take a bite from the apple in Genesis. How else does one explain such things as unisex bathrooms or reality programming? Heck, in the weeks leading up to the Great Revelation, there was even an underground movement with a website called Bloodcopy.com that had begun to expose the existence of vampires to those who would listen. And with Daddy having his own suspicions that vampires may be a reality, not a fiction, I can't say I was shocked when I saw the news that night. In fact, I was elated. Daddy was right–nay, all of Christianity was right–we were facing down the barrel of the End Times and things were about to get good. Jesus Christ's promise of a Second Coming was about to be fulfilled (JC, come on down!).

YOU WIN A FEW POINTS HERE, STEVE. VAMPIRES DID BANKROLL TRU BLOOD. THE FINANCING OF THE DEVELOPMENT OF THE SYNTHETIC BEVERAGE HAS QUITE A SORDID HISTORY, THOUGH. THE JAPANESE VAMPIRE COMMUNITY IS A QUAGMIRE OF POLITICS AND CRIME BEST LEFT UNINVESTIGATED.

Yet who knew that Armageddon would begin in a laboratory in Japan? Without the work of the scientific community at the Yakonomo Corporation, the Japanese enterprise that developed the synthetic blood that became Tru Blood, the world would not have confirmation of vampires. When Yakonomo's invention of the blood substitute was first unveiled to the public, I thought this revolutionary substance could pave the way for miracles in the medical field. But, and this is a biggie, it is my belief the project was actually secretly bankrolled by Japanese vampires!* Otherwise the FDA (probably in league with vampires as well) should approve it for use in blood transfusions! My point is the government still hasn't allowed for the use of Tru Blood in hospitals, but walk into any five-and-dime on the corner of Main Street, USA, and you'll see it sitting in huge, radiant, red vending machines inviting every vampire in a five-mile radius to stop by your town like it was a perfectly acceptable and safe thing for the community! Add to that the fact that vampires were organizing online via their own website called "The Reverent Ones" (ha!), calling for the support of the mainstream movement months before the announcement of Tru Blood, and you have what I call a conspiracy of biblical proportions.

Nan Flanagan went on national TV, backed by Tru Blood, and told the American people that vampires were walking amongst us, had been doing so for centuries, and yet we had absolutely nothing to fear. The hypocrisy is sickening. If there are "no recorded attacks on humans" (as she has stated on Real Time with Bill Maher), then WHY did it take the invention of a blood substitute to allow them to come out of the coffin in the first place? Sometimes I feel like the only sane person left on this planet. *You and me, both, sister.*

Japan harbors some of the oldest known vampires on the planet; see H.W. Alan Jackson's Bloodlines: Satan's Family Tree for a fascinating history of vampire origins. You'll also find out who was really behind the bombing of Pearl Harbor!

*Not to be confused with Elizabeth J. Jennings's "anthropological study," The First Disease: The Evolution of Vampirism, which traces vampires back to a rare blood disease found in an ancestor of the Japanese macaque. Hey lady, you really believe vampires descended from sick monkeys? Give. Me. A. Break.

VAMPIRE POLITICS AND GOVERNMENT

Considering the chaotic and violent nature of vampires, I was thoroughly surprised to discover that they have their own legal system with crimes and punishments, and even some checks and balances.

Sheriffs and Magisters

In this quasi-cabinet, "magister" is the highest form of office a vampire can hold, at least that I'm aware of. Beneath the magister operate countless vampire "sheriffs," divided across "Areas," or territories, who work to keep tabs on any and all vampire business, both legal and illegal.

Sheriffs don't just "keep tabs." When Eric was the sheriff of Area 5, before Miss Stackhouse came into our lives and destroyed everything awesome about my maker, he was a force in vampire society. Vampires were so scared of his wrath, they toed the line just to avoid him.

KNOWN ENEMY

NAME: Jorje Alonso de San Diego

SPECIES: Vampire

AGE: Born in 1462, made vampire in 1525

STATUS: ~~Active~~ *Beheaded*

OCCUPATION: Magister

MAKER: Unknown

KNOWN PROGENY: None

The Justice System

The most offensive crime a vampire can commit within his community is killing another vampire. He or she will be put on trial, whereby the magister will hand down some form of punishment. Although the discipline can vary, the severity remains constant. A typical sentence for killing another vampire is five years in a silver-lined coffin, which not only results in emaciation and skin damage, but oftentimes leads to unmitigated insanity. Other punishments involve removal of fangs, which will cause a vampire to starve for three to four months until his teeth grow back, or forcing the accused to turn a human of the magister's choice into a vampire. This form of punishment is used most often in cases where the accused is of the more . . . sensitive persuasion. The sentencing seems somewhat arbitrary, but I suppose our legal system could be viewed that way too. I mean, a human judge actually saw fit to slap Senator Larry Craig with a disorderly conduct charge when the poor man was just trying to use the bathroom at the Minneapolis-St. Paul airport!

Another well-known crime in the vampire community is being photographed or videotaped while feeding on humans. If caught, the vampire will face execution, a.k.a. the True Death. I find this law particularly disgusting, because it does not actually discourage vampires from feeding on humans, it simply encourages that they do it behind closed doors. Further evidence of the farce that is Tru Blood, if you ask me.

There also seem to be a few "codes," not necessarily written laws but moral standards, by which vampires abide–if we are to believe that vampires have any sort of moral standards at all. They do not feed on another vampire's human (if it weren't amongst creatures of Satan, I might regard this as mildly chivalrous). A vampire just has to tell another that "the human is mine" in order for the relationship to be understood. They also purport that abstaining from feeding on children is among these codes, but do they really expect us to believe they don't eat our babies? That's hogwash!

It's remarkably true. We don't eat your annoying offspring. They're too pasty and pudgy. Vampires that feed on children are shunned like human pedophiles. They become pariahs, ostracized and tortured by their own kind.

*I resent that. I take **very** good care of the Fangtasia dancers–each and every one of them has access to health care. That's more than I can say about the moral standards of most human businesses.*

Vampire Monarchy

Operating in conjunction with sheriffs and magisters are the vampire monarchs. These crowned monsters may have reigned over their kingdom of bloodsuckers at some point in history, but now, much like the queen of England, these royals are mere figureheads with too much time and money on their hands. According to Hinter's book Decrypting Vampires, vampire kings and queens date back to Byzantium and Prussia and perhaps even Canaanite times. These days, monarch territories–at least here in the good ol' US of A–are divided by states. A vampire named Queen Sophie-Anne reigns over Louisiana, and none other than Russell Edgington himself lounges atop the throne of Mississippi. And of course, my personal enemy Stan Baker was crowned king of Texas after rescuing Godric from my church. Now one would assume sheriffs would answer to these fellows, but from what I've ascertained, these lazy loafs have little to no say in how their territories are governed, and adjudication is left to the office of magister. King Compton spends his nights playing Wii golf, Russell Edgington just strikes me as a madman with rich taste (but rather nice hair), and Stan is nothing more than a renegade cowpuncher with an itchy trigger finger. For all intents and purposes, the monarchs are just remnants of a bygone era, desperately clinging to the ghost of its heyday. Kind of like the Kennedys, or video stores.

AND DECORATING HIS MANSION WITH EVERY LAST KNOWN
ANIMAL SKIN TO BE FOUND ON THE AFRICAN CONTINENT.
I THINK HE'S SINGLE-HANDEDLY PUT
ZEBRAS ON THE ENDANGERED SPECIES LIST.

KNOWN ENEMY

NAME Sophie-Anne LeClerq

SPECIES Vampire

AGE Made vampire in 1488

STATUS Deceased

OCCUPATION Monarch

MAKER Unknown

KNOWN PROGENY None

NOT

IF STEVE NEWLIN COULD DREAM UP THE AUTHORITY, THEN THE AUTHORITY'S NOT DOING A VERY GOOD JOB.

Secret Vampire Council

Now I'm not a genius, per se, but I'm smart enough to know that there's a missing piece to this puzzle. Who oversees all of these different departments? The public would assume it's the American Vampire League (AVL), but that has only been recently formed to promote mainstreaming, with Nan Flanagan acting as head of vampire public relations. Given this fractured, somewhat confusing system, there can only be one conclusion: there is a shadow government hidden behind the magisters and sheriffs and monarchs, behind the AVL and its Vampire Rights Amendment, perhaps even beneath the surface of the earth. A secret vampire mafia that truly runs the show, spends oodles of (stolen) money on the vampire agenda, and if I'm being totally honest, probably keeps cells full of humans waiting around to be fed upon. If I were a gambling man, I would say there's somewhere from six to eight officers, under the auspices of one central dictator-perhaps even Satan himself. I can picture them now, sitting at some big conference table in their underground lair, drinking blood out of decanters and plotting the enslavement of mankind. Sometimes Sarah would think I was full of crazy conspiracy theories, but I just have a gut feeling about this one. Unfortunately, I doubt my theories will ever be confirmed. Whether or not this shadow government exists will probably never be revealed to humans. Vampires have had no qualms about keeping us in the dark for centuries, so it's safe to assume they'll continue to do so.

WITH ROMAN GONE, SALOME IN CHARGE, AND BILL ACTING LIKE A WEIRDO, THE AUTHORITY WILL BE MAKING HEADLINES FROM CNN TO THE WEEKLY WORLD NEWS ANY NIGHT NOW . . .

THE MAINSTREAMING MOVEMENT AND THE AMERICAN VAMPIRE LEAGUE

Abel had Cain. Jesus has Lucifer. I have Nan Flanagan.

Very little is known about Nan Flanagan, spokesvampire (can I really say "spokes<u>person</u>"?) for the American Vampire League. Flanagan is significant, because for most people, barring those who were the victims of vampire attacks during what I now refer to as "The Dark Days" (the time when humanity was ignorant to the existence of vampires), Nan was the first vampire that humans laid eyes on. And I bet she just ate that right up like it was a freshly-slaughtered babe ripped from its moonlit cradle (sorry for the violent rhetoric, I've just had a particularly infuriating conversation with Sarah's divorce lawyer). Nan Flanagan clearly <u>loves the spotlight</u>. I'm not sure who she was in her former life (the AVL refuses to comment, claiming it is a violation of her "vampire rights"), but I assert without equivocation that Nan Flanagan is the Whore of Babylon in this one.

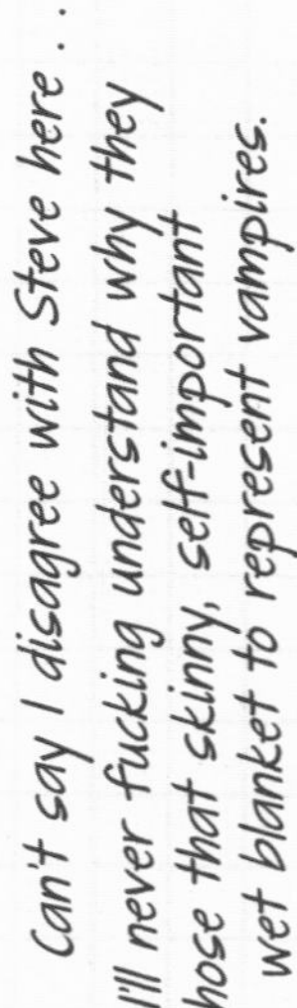

This much is known: While Nan is the voice of the vampire public, she is not its sole policy maker. She does not publicly claim the title of magister, sheriff, or monarch. This begs the question, <u>To whom does she answer?</u> Which in itself begs the question, <u>Who is really governing the vampire community?</u> Perhaps this will convince you of my Secret Vampire Council theory.

KNOWN ENEMY

NOTE

NAME Nan Flanagan

SPECIES Vampire

AGE Unknown

STATUS ~~Active~~ → DESTROYED BY YOURS TRULY

OCCUPATION Spokesperson for the AVL

MAKER Unknown

KNOWN PROGENY None

The AVL is just the public face of the vampire mainstreaming movement. On the surface they appear to be a benign group, claiming peaceful cohabitation with the human species. Beneath the charade, they are planning a complete global takeover. I have broken down their agenda into a two-part strategy I call "EVADE and INVADE":

1. EVADE: Lull the public into trusting vampires. The AVL wants to keep the public's attitudes toward vampires docile and liberal, while secretly regarding us as sheep they are fattening up for the slaughter.

2. INVADE: The AVL is working hard to shove vampire rights legislation down the bloated throat of our government in order to make it more legal for vampires to infiltrate the human race. Some of the keynotes of the so-called Vampire Rights Amendment (VRA) include:

   - VOTING RIGHTS FOR VAMPIRES
   - VAMPIRE/HUMAN MARRIAGE RIGHTS
   - VAMPIRE HOSPITAL VISITATION RIGHTS FOR LIVING HUMAN RELATIVES
   - THE BANNING OF ALL ANTI-VAMPIRE WEAPONS, INCLUDING BUT NOT LIMITED TO: STAKES, SILVER CHAINS, AND BOTH WOODEN AND SILVER BULLETS. Maybe next they should just ban the sunlight?
   - COMPLETE EXEMPTION OF PREVIOUS LIFE. I don't know all the legal mumbo jumbo here, but basically this would mean that a vampire's "previous human life" would for all intents and purposes be erased from record by the government. This law would make a vampire's legal birthdate the night they were turned. They would not be legally forced to admit to their true age, nationalization, or background. However, they can legally keep their money by automatically being considered, by law, their sole inheritor upon being made a vampire. Worst of all, any previous criminal record or prison internment would be completely eradicated once they had been turned. Not sure about you, but this sounds like a really appealing "get out of jail free card" for murderers and child molesters–just the kind of recruits vampires want on their side!

Nan Flanagan and I have gone toe-to-toe on many occasions over the airwaves. I have to say that she may be able to keep her cool (hard not to when you're a walking corpse), but she's nothing but a bag of liberal hot air. When PHASE 2 of my plan kicks in, I'll come gunning after Ms. Flanagan first. And I do mean, "gunning." I look forward to the day I can reintroduce her to her true maker in all of His Glorious Light.

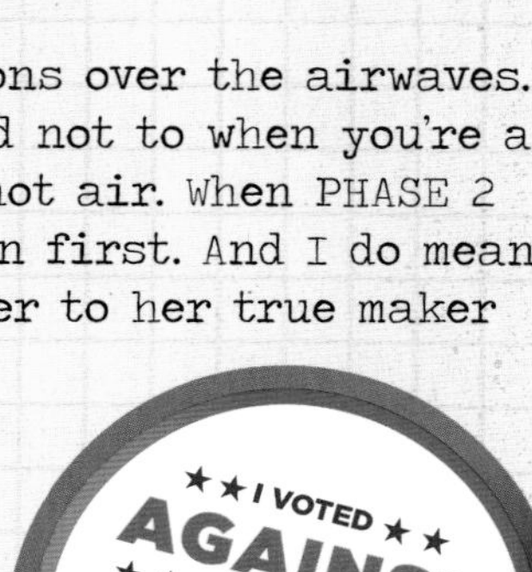

★★ I VOTED ★★
AGAINST
★★★ THE ★★★
VRA!
I HOPE YOU DID TOO, OTHERWISE YOU'LL HAVE HELL TO PAY!

We're even more beautiful *after* sunset . . .
Begin your eternal life together in Vermont.
Welcoming Humans & Vampires together
VERMONT
TOURISM BOARD

Your Love will last Forever
The cake will go quickly.
CAKES BY VANESSA
DESSERTS FOR ALL OCCASIONS
Proudly serving the human and vampire communities

It is an abomination, but not for any moral or religious reasons. Why would a vampire possibly want to MARRY a human? That would make them spouses, partners, equals . . . I prefer my humans in this order: entertainment, food, then pets.

INTERSPECIES MARRIAGE AND WHY IT'S AN ABOMINATION

As if vampires weren't asking for enough-equal protection under the law, voting rights, property rights-there's a new movement gaining momentum, looking to legalize interspecies marriage throughout the entire country! Sure, a few delinquent states have already jumped on the bandwagon of this ridiculous notion, but it's widely agreed upon in this country that this is a dangerous and profoundly amoral road to go down. I cannot possibly express the supreme importance of preserving the sanctity of marriage and protecting the traditional definition: the unique union between ONE MAN and ONE WOMAN.

So were you the woman in your marriage, Steve?

To point out the obvious, vampires are not men and women. They are the memories of men and women, now dead and devoid of any true human characteristics. In fact, marriage vows end with "until death do you part." God tells us that a marriage is over when a husband or wife dies. Right there from the get-go, vamps are voided by God, since they're already dead!

And before anyone starts shouting about redefining death as "True Death," which has already been proposed by flaming liberals on the bozo-sphere, let's get to the most important matter in this debate: vampires cannot procreate! Females lack ovaries and fallopian tubes, and males cannot produce little swimmers. And is it not but for the children that we uphold the statutes of holy matrimony? I realize I'm not a paragon of excellence in this arena. My own marriage has regrettably crumbled, but I wanted children. Sarah said it would be an offense against God's beautiful creation if she ruined her body before she turned 30, so she was making us wait. If it weren't for her vanity, little Barnabas Teddy could have been starting preschool this fall! So she must take responsibility in the eyes of the Lord for that, as well as for stepping outside our marriage to have sexual relations with Jason Stackhouse.

To get back to the matter at hand, one must rely on the facts. Vermont, the first state to legalize interspecies marriage, has seen some scary statistics since it opened its doors to the calamitous couples. It seems that the institution of marriage itself has suffered at the hands of this new enactment. Studies prove that the promotion of nontraditional marriage has increased divorce rates and encouraged traditional couples not to marry, which has resulted in a spike in the numbers of babies born out of wedlock. How are children supposed to succeed in these broken homes? Are the children not our future? Shall we not teach them well and let them lead the way? If we as adult humans cannot protect the sanctity of the God-fearing family, how can we possibly expect our children to become anything but terrorists, couch potatoes, or sluts?

Furthermore, what would a vampire/human marriage look like in the long term? The human will inevitably age and then die, as God intended us to, while the vampire will live on, untouched by wrinkles or years. What then? Is the vampire free to marry again, and again, and again?

The only grounds upon which these misguided activists fight for interspecies marriage rights are "love" and "emotional bonds" -but these have never been requirements of marriage. Look at Sarah and me: love and emotional bonding never proved to be relevant! But perhaps most importantly, interspecies marriage would undermine the human condition and invite corruption into our relationships with each other and with God. And as a man of the cloth, and an air-breathing Homo sapiens, I just can't let that happen.

VAMPIRE SYMPATHIZERS

> "Marvel not at this, for the hour is coming, in which all that are in the graves shall hear the sound of His Voice, and shall come forth; they that have done good, unto the resurrection of life; they that have done evil, unto the resurrection of damnation."
>
> —John 5:28-29

Powerful words. John tells us in the Bible that when the final Day of Judgment comes, those who are good and believe in Christ shall rise from the dead and receive everlasting life. Those who are wicked and turn against Christ will also rise from the dead, but unto the life of the damned.

Now who does that sound like?

From this passage alone we can see that the life of a vampire, although reincarnated through resurrection, is not Christ-like. It is the life of damnation. There is a passage to everlasting life, but it is through the love of Christ and Christ alone. I pity the poor vampire sympathizer-a human who fights for the rights of vampires-because they have been misled into thinking that vampires are equal to mankind, when in fact they have already been damned by God.

Sure, vampires may seem "cool" or "sexy." It may sound "modern" to join the vampire movement. You turn on any cable channel, pick up any young adult book, or hop into any theatre in any multiplex in any state across the United States and Hollywood keeps shelling out the same lies: Vamps are just like us. Vamps need to be loved. Vamps are capable of loving. Vamps are capable of marriage. Vamps are capable of salvation. Well, that's because Hollywood is the great megaphone of the devil himself, and the media moguls who sold their souls for back end and box office percentages don't want you to know that the only salvation comes through Christ. And, it's free!

So what do we do with vampire sympathizers like Sookie Stackhouse? Or the vampire in Kill Creek, Colorado who was just elected mayor by human citizens? Or the Democratic U.S. senators and congressmen that are fighting for vampire rights? You keep preaching and hoping that they hear the good word. But when they move to take what is good and righteous from you and yours, well, you tell them to go to hell (and send them there early, if needed). Now, I don't condone the capturing and killing of human beings. Some are meek, having been tempted by loneliness, fear, desperation, isolation, and ignorance. They can still be saved. But others are too far gone. Most of these vampire sympathizers, no matter how they were wooed to the dark side, are now TERRORISTS IN LEAGUE WITH SATAN. For them, it is simply too late. And in these instances, action must be taken.

We even pump our own gas!
Sorry, I've been reading too much US Weekly lately . . .

A VAMPIRE'S TAKE ON VAMPIRE SYMPATHIZERS

LOOK, I GREW UP DURING THE GOOD OLD DAYS OF HUNTING, SCREWING, AND KILLING. WILLING DONORS BORE ME. MOST SYMPATHIZERS ARE IDIOTS WHO CAN'T HOLD DOWN A REGULAR JOB, LET ALONE ADVANCE THE RIGHTS OF VAMPIRE AMERICANS. BUT WHEN IT COMES TO MY BUSINESS, THEY'RE A NECESSARY EVIL. AND I HAVE TO ADMIT, AS TINY AND PETTY AS HUMANS ARE, IT'S SOMEWHAT AMUSING TO SEE THE IMPACT OUR EXISTENCE HAS HAD ON THEIR CULTURE. THE COSTUMES CAN GET A LITTLE OUTLANDISH AND PREDICTABLE, AND FEW HAVE THE BODY FOR THEM, BUT I'D BE LYING IF I SAID IT ISN'T REFRESHING TO SEE THE REPRESSION OF THE LAST FEW CENTURIES FINALLY LOOSEN UP A BIT.

NOW, I PERSONALLY DON'T GIVE A SHIT ABOUT MAINSTREAMING, BUT IT HASN'T BEEN SO BAD. I'VE MADE VERY FEW SACRIFICES AND I ENJOY THE RESPECT THAT COMES WITH RUNNING MY BUSINESS OUT IN THE OPEN. AND I HAVE TO ADMIT THAT WHEN I'M SITTING ON MY THRONE, LOOKING OUT INTO THE SEA OF FOOLS BEFORE ME, AFTER A LIFETIME IN THE SHADOWS, IT FEELS GOOD TO BE WANTED.

WHAT WE
NEED IS SOME
KIND OF PRISON FOR VAMPS...

A VAMP CAMP!!

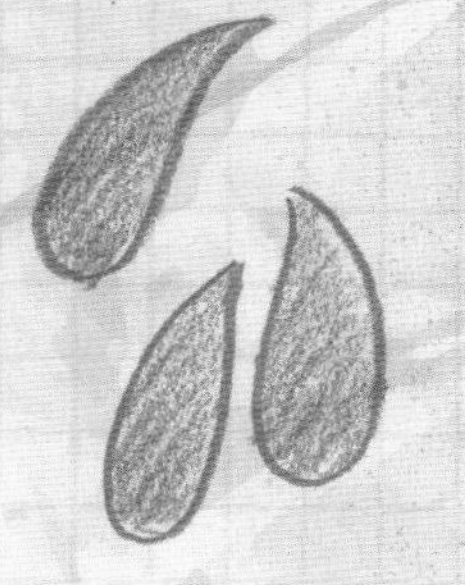

Fangbangers

Steve set out to write a book about freaks, but he left out the biggest fruit loops of them all: FANGBANGERS. They think they fit in around our kind, in our nests, at our bars, but they stick out like crooked fangs. We can smell their desperation from miles away, and their menial attempt to find a place in the world is pathetic. Reality is harsh, but there's a reason Martha Dumptruck wasn't a Heather.

The fangbanger culture breaks down kind of like this:

<u>CLOSET BANGERS:</u>
Typically your polished politician, cruising park bathrooms and rent-a-vamp websites for clandestine kicks.

<u>LEATHER BOYS:</u>
These guys look like goth bikers, only they've probably never even touched a motorcycle in their lives. They usually outfit themselves with fake leather from the mall, and underneath all that black mascara, they're more sensitive than that fussy Merlotte's waitress Arlene.

<u>SORORITY GIRLS:</u>
Skinny legs, big boobs, small brains. The kind of girls with overprotective daddies, these fangbangers have no idea what kind of danger they're getting themselves into . . .

<u>UNHAPPY HOUSEWIVES:</u>
The name says it all. Most of them keep their wedding rings on to assure potential suitors that they're looking for a no-strings-attached arrangement. Four out of ten unhappy housewives find themselves in the next category after their first fangbang . . .

DIVORCEES:

Newly single folks, often shlubby and hopeless, looking to fill that lonely space that was once occupied by a loved one. Nothing like the taste of heartbreak, right?

HEP-D CATS:

These nasty humans carry the blood-borne virus and disguise themselves as fangbangers in an effort to lure and infect vampires. The tell-tale signs? Dark circles under their eyes and metallic-tasting blood.

JOCKS:

Athletes posing as fangbangers, looking to score some V. Apparently it helps their football stats, not that anyone really gives a shit about amateur sports.

FANG SKANKS:

Super-trashy fangirls who have taken their obsession with our kind way too far for comfort. They hang around Fangtasia every night, rarely seeing the light of day. These gals only sleep with vampires, no matter the make or mold, and their necks and inner thighs are generally riddled with bite marks. You know Ginger? She's a fang skank.

THE STACKHOUSE CLAN

Speaking of fangbangers . . .

November 8

The Stackhouse family tree has been rooted in Renard Parish since 1834, when public record shows Jonas Stackhouse settled in the small village of Bon Temps. His descendants, Sookie and Jason Stackhouse, have been at the center of major vampire-related action ever since the night vampire Bill Compton walked into Miss Stackhouse's life. How he so quickly converted a once sweet child of God into an evil whore of Satan is a testimony to the corruptive influence of vampires. From what I can tell, she was the kind of girl who wore a cross around her neck, attended church on a regular basis, and minded her own business . . . up until the moment she got mixed up with bloodsuckers. Her older brother, Jason, on the other hand, has always been a bit of a lost sheep, which is what brought him to me in the first place. Or so I thought.

Sookie and Jason were orphaned at a young age when their parents Corbett and Michelle Stackhouse drowned in a flash flood. The children were taken in by their grandparents, Earl and Adele Stackhouse, and grew up surrounded by other surviving family members, including their cousin Hadley Hale, Corbett's sister Linda Stackhouse-Hale, and Adele's brother Bartlett.

For someone as paranoid as Steve, I'm surprised it didn't occur to him that Sookie's parents may not have died in a natural disaster, but may have been killed by yet another vampire with a hard-on for Sookie.

Jason and Sookie's adolescent experiences could not have been more different, despite being bonded by blood. Jason was a beloved, all-American QB-1 heartthrob, whose sexual escapades I can only imagine began at an early age and under inappropriate circumstances (I saved myself for my wedding night, despite Sarah's insistence that the "back door" wouldn't count as losing our virginity). Jason's six-pack of charisma made him popular with guys and gals alike, and has continued to serve him well into adulthood; he was the center of everyone's attention the whole time he was at camp! Despite his naiveté, Jason is a born leader and a cold killer. He could have been the greatest Soldier of the Sun to ever swing a silver-tipped stake.

NOW WHO'S BEING NAIVE? JASON IS A WITLESS MEAT-SACK WHO DIDN'T INHERIT ANY OF THE QUALITIES THAT MAKE HIS SISTER SO SPECIAL.

Bon Temps Gazette

ACROSS

1. Four-time Renard Parish Fair Winner for Best Pig.
6. How many biscuits to an order at Marty's Biscuit Shack on Highway 49?
8. The Frog Capital of the World.
19. Vampires drink this to stay alive.
36. Our great state was named after King Louis _______.
38. Edna Knowles' son Howie played "Cop #4" in this 2002 Hollywood blockbuster.
48. Oldest item on the Merlotte's menu.
49. The late Reverend Torrey's favorite sermon topic.
50. French word for slow-moving river.
54. Bon Temps is French for "Good _______".

DOWN

1. Crawfish Capital of the World.
5. State flower.
16. Adele Stackhouse was the direct descendant of this local celebrity.
17. State bird.
18. Other states call parishes this.
21. This factory was located just outside Mansfield and shut down in 1994 due to vermin.
24. Lynne Dearborne married retired Sheriff Bud Dearborne at this banquet hall in Natchitoches.
29. Oldest city in Tangipahoa Parish.
32. State just north of Claiborne Parish.
44. "If it's not Renard Parish, it's not _______"
45. Governor of Louisiana.

I had high hopes that Jason would lead the Fellowship into PHASE 2, as an affable, sexy, funny, capable, talented, and good-hearted public face for our mission of good. He is God's perfect specimen, really, so who better to spread His good word to the world? I thought he was sent to me as a reward for keeping my daddy's work going, so you can imagine my devastation to learn that he had actually been sent ahead of his sister as a spy to help the Dallas vampires rescue Godric. A few days after the dust from "The Incident" had settled, I locked myself in my room for a good day and cried. I'm not ashamed to admit it. Jason was more than a friend or pupil to me, more than a brother . . . he was like a soul-brother. I loved him more than I loved Sarah at times. I just don't understand why he'd betray me in so many ways.

I'll tell you what, though. There's something of me still left inside Stackhouse. Before he came to me, he was scared, aimless, even accused of murder at one point! Now? He's on his way to becoming a deputy sheriff of Bon Temps! I followed him to one of his training courses just yesterday, and from the view in my binoculars, he seemed to be at the top of his class-which doesn't surprise me one bit. He may have been a snake in the grass, but I'll be damned if he hasn't started to turn his life around. As angry as

I am for what happened, I'm still proud of him. And there will always be room for Jason in my heart.

Sookie, however, can burn in hell. I had heard of a mind-reading waitress arriving in Dallas through my own spy, Hugo Ayers, who had infiltrated Stan Baker's vampire circle to find evidence of my father's assassination. When Hugo came up short, I thought that a fangbanging telepath might just be the key to solving the mystery of Daddy's death. Sookie proved to be a formidable foe with friends in high places, but in the end I got what I wanted out of Stan: a confession that he and the Dallas vamps killed my daddy. Did it make me feel better about how Daddy died? Not really. I already knew he was a divine martyr, having sacrificed himself for God's army. But it sure as heck reignited my fire of vengeance to win this war once and for all.

After "The Incident" at the Fellowship, I followed Sookie back to Bon Temps, to see what kind of crack she crawled out of. Her place was a dump; it was covered in mud and there was some kind of bohemian-satanic revelry taking place. I made sure to keep my distance. I returned to her hometown a few more times to find it cleaned up and normal enough on the surface, but the place remains a haven for supernatural activity. Since leaving my church, Sookie has been involved with the usual vampire peanut gallery, as well as expanding her horizons to include dealings with werewolves and even the vampire king of Mississippi! She disappeared shortly thereafter, though; I've completely lost trace of her. Maybe she died, or maybe she's lying low, plotting her next move in hiding. In her absence, her home has gotten a much-needed makeover and the whole town seems to have settled down, suggesting to me that it is not Bon Temps that is the epicenter of Satan's energy, but perhaps Sookie Stackhouse herself. After all, she may not even be human, given those mind-reading skills . . . Luckily, the good humans of Renard Parish have Jason to keep them safe, whatever happens. I know I'd feel safe in those arms.

Maybe it's time I gave him a call?

and witches, and faeries, and rednecks . . .

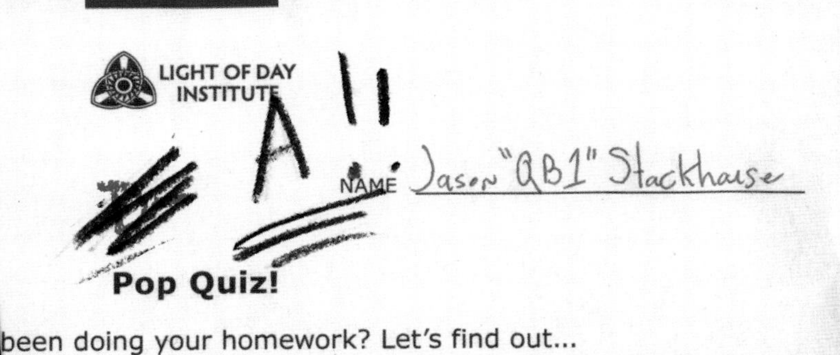

NAME Jason "QB1" Stackhause

Pop Quiz!

...been doing your homework? Let's find out...

1. Who founded the Fellowship of the Sun and what is his relation to Steve and Sarah Newlin?

   The Fellowship of the SUN was founded by Steve's dad, but I can't remember the dude's name. I think it was Timothy? OR Teddy? Starts with a T.

2. What does your FOTS promise ring stand for?

   We got engaged to the Fellowship and to the Newlins. Only we're not gonna get married. It's kind of confusing.

3. Why do vampires exist? Who sent them to Earth?

   God's evil twin put vampires on the planet to punish us for all the sex I've been having.

4. What is the fastest way to defeat a vampire?

   Wooden Bullet to the heart. Boom!

5. What has been your favorite activity at camp and why?

   I loved playing capture the flag, because I'm real good at it and because I kicked Luke's ~~ass~~ butt.

PRAISE HIS LIGHT!

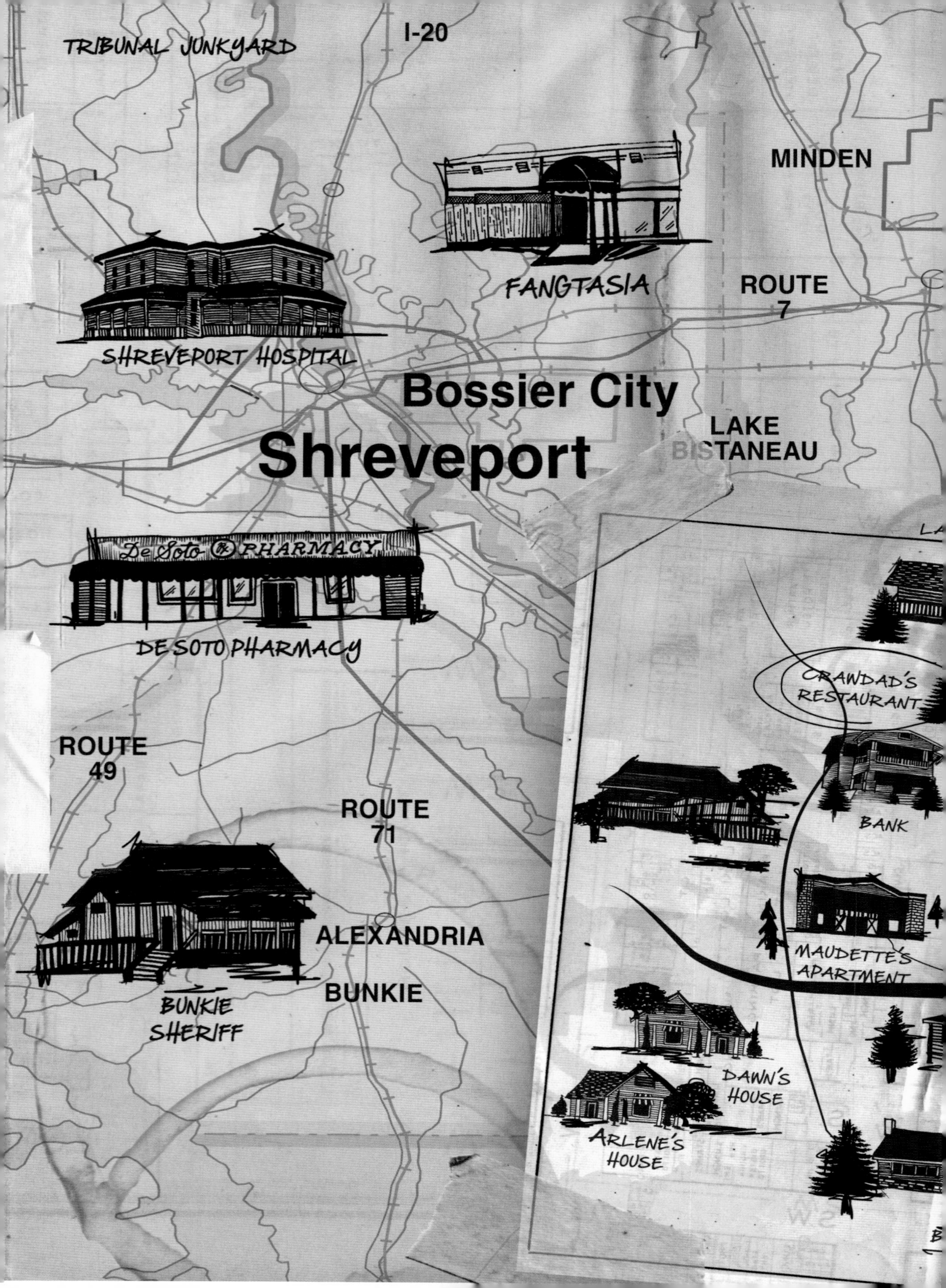

TRIBUNAL JUNKYARD
I-20
MINDEN
FANGTASIA
ROUTE
7
SHREVEPORT HOSPITAL
Bossier City
LAKE
BISTANEAU
Shreveport
De Soto PHARMACY
DE SOTO PHARMACY
CRAWDAD'S
RESTAURANT
ROUTE
49
ROUTE
71
BANK
ALEXANDRIA
BUNKIE
BUNKIE
SHERIFF
MAUDETTE'S
APARTMENT
DAWN'S
HOUSE
ARLENE'S
HOUSE

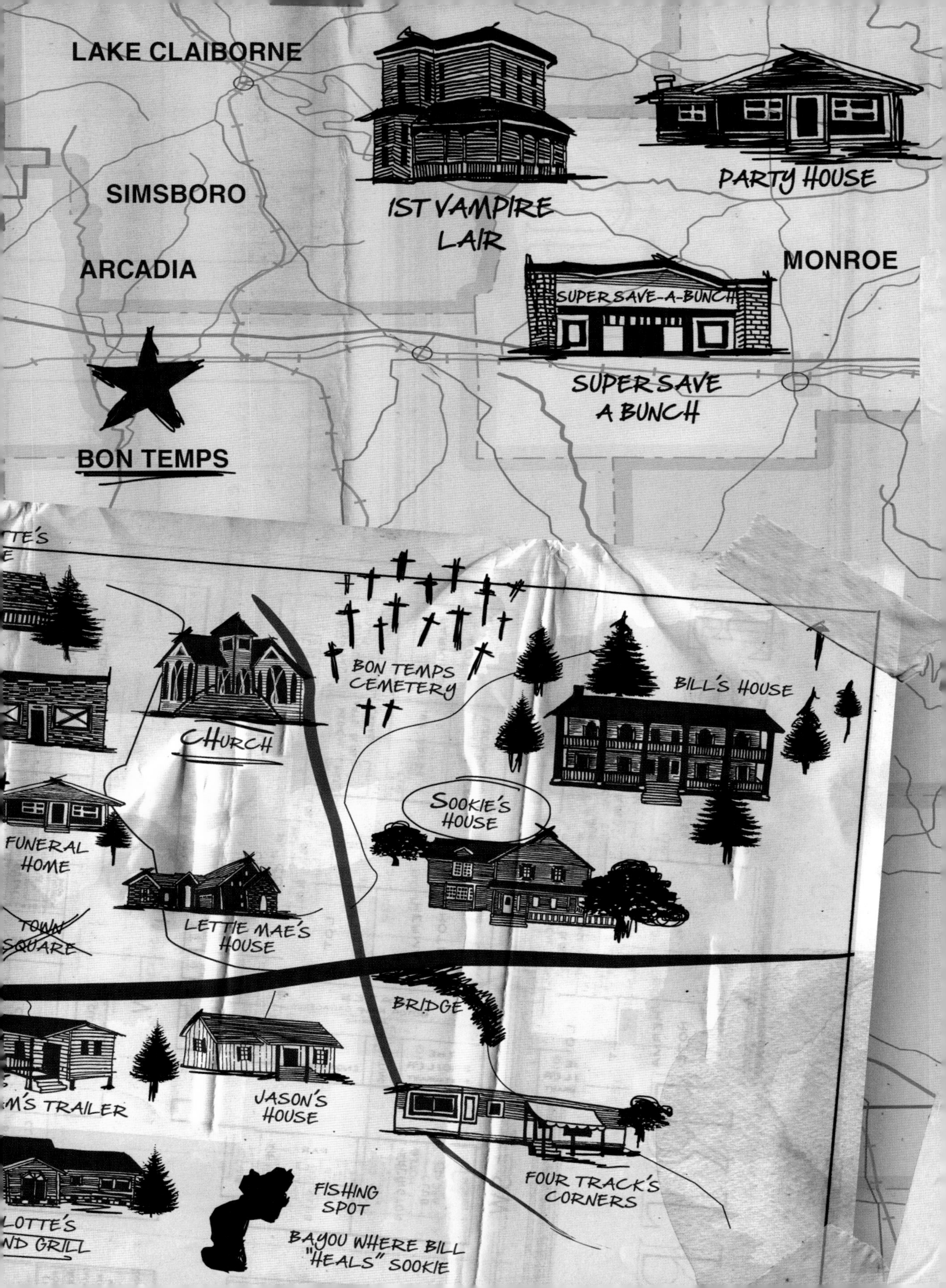

LAKE CLAIBORNE
SIMSBORO
ARCADIA
BON TEMPS
1ST VAMPIRE LAIR
PARTY HOUSE
MONROE
SUPER SAVE-A-BUNCH
SUPER SAVE A BUNCH
CHURCH
BON TEMPS CEMETERY
BILL'S HOUSE
SOOKIE'S HOUSE
FUNERAL HOME
LETTIE MAE'S HOUSE
TOWN SQUARE
BRIDGE
JASON'S HOUSE
FOUR TRACK'S CORNERS
FISHING SPOT
BAYOU WHERE BILL "HEALS" SOOKIE

RESIDENTS OF BON TEMPS

The following residents of Renard Parish are known accomplices of the Stackhouse clan.

TARA THORNTON

Sookie's childhood friend, daughter of churchgoing Lettie Mae Thornton and all-around troublemaker who could use some divine intervention. Let's just say without it, things aren't going to end well for this one.

Tara's divine intervention came in a pale yellow Walmart sweatsuit. She's mine now.

SHERIFF ANDY BELLEFLEUR

Recently appointed sheriff of Bon Temps, Andy has taken Jason under his wing to help him blossom into the man I know he can be. Despite being a recovering V addict, he seems to keep things on the pretty straight and narrow.

TERRY BELLEFLEUR

Andy's cousin and short-order cook at Merlotte's, Terry served his country in Iraq for two tours.

ARLENE FOWLER

Currently engaged to Terry Bellefleur, Arlene's been married too many times to count, previously to the misunderstood hero Drew Marshall (aka Rene Lenier). She has two children, Coby and Lisa, and is currently pregnant with her third.

She already popped out that future redneck. I wish these Southern bumpkins would use some protection.

AND THEY'RE WORRIED ABOUT THE VAMPIRE POPULATION GROWING?

A cross-dressing, homosexual, drug-dealing short-order cook. I've seen his online work, and I do not approve.

LAFAYETTE REYNOLDS

HOYT FORTENBERRY:

Once an upstanding member of Bon Temps' road crew, Hoyt has recently been lured to the dark side by vampire Jessica Hamby. He is now a fangbanger, ~~living in sin with his girlfriend~~. I pray for his mother, Maxine.

Drilling for oil in Alaska

I've heard this single mother of two is a practicing Wiccan, but this rumor has yet to be confirmed. Otherwise, she's a Merlotte's waitress and appears to be mostly harmless.

HOLLY CLEARY

THE SIX STEPS TO HEAVEN

While many people have kicked family members out of their homes, disowned children, and estranged themselves from loved ones, I, Steve Newlin, will not turn my back on fallen fangbangers looking to put the pieces of their lives back together. God is forgiving, shall I not be too? It's important to make the distinction, however, between fangbangers hoping to repent for their sins and reintegrate into normal, healthy society, and those, like Sookie Stackhouse, who are happy with their vampire-loving ways. I will not open my doors to people looking to make a mockery of God's love or of my beloved church and I have no qualms inducing bodily harm where appropriate. Even in God's good world, there are necessary evils.

I've spent the past few years devising and developing a rehabilitation program for recovering fangbangers (also known as "vamp addicts"), to help them get their lives back on track and reopen those gates to heaven. It's a lot like a 12-step program, only it's more efficient: we've only got 6 steps! Who is the program for? Anyone and everyone who's been glamoured into the vampire way of life. Fangbanging knows no boundaries; this kind of addiction has affected people from all different places, cultures, and socioeconomic backgrounds. We offer both outpatient and residential options, but ultimately, the program and its tenets are the same. Residential treatment is recommended for people in crisis mode, who have little to no resources to fall back on.* The outpatient program is geared towards less severe addictions, and is often revisited by already recovered addicts looking to renew the vows of their new lifestyle. We at Six Steps to Heaven strive to help people overcome addiction and break the cycle of dependence that has set them on the road to hell. We also work to provide program graduates with the tools they need to start a new life so they can avoid falling back into their old ways. The most important thing to know before sending a loved one our way is that we cannot fix them if they do not want to be fixed. Fangbangers have to enlist on their own accord. They have to want to get better. Otherwise, like vampires themselves, they are doomed.

* I am of course referring to resources like coping mechanisms, emotional outlets, and trusted caretakers. As far as financial resources go, we require a $900 deposit fee to join the program.

ATTENTION YOUTH MEMBERS:

LIGHT OF DAY INSTITUT

LEADERSHI
CONFERENC

*Only $1200**

"There's no price for salvation"

CONTACT:
REVEREND STEVE OR
SARAH NEWLIN FOR
FUTHER DETAILS.

* Room, Board, and Transportation are not covered, this is just the cost of class fees.

The
Six Steps
to
HEAVEN

by Reverend Steve Newlin

1. Admitting you have a problem

Easier said than done! It takes a lot of courage to come forward and say, I'm addicted to vampires or I'm addicted to V. People like to believe they're in control of their lives, that their habit is manageable. Unfortunately, they are often too blinded by the devil to see that they have totally lost control. If you can admit to yourself and to those around you that you have a problem, you can take the next step towards solving it.

It also takes a lot of courage to admit you're a showboating idiot, but we're cheering you on, Steve.

2. Pledging abstinence

On your first day in the program, you will be required to sign a contract stating you will abstain from any and all vampire interaction and V ingestion. Anyone who chooses to break this contract will be promptly removed from the program and kicked out of the facility. Trust us when we say it's for your own good and for the good of those around you!

3. Accepting Jesus Christ as your savior

We cannot save you if you cannot save yourself. This is a unique opportunity to open up your heart to the Man who can heal those metaphorical bite marks and transform your soul into a well of righteousness.

4. Making amends

I have yet to meet an ex-fangbanger who, while addicted, didn't do some serious harm to the people in his or her life. In order to move forward, you need to make peace with your past. This involves compiling a list of all of your wrongdoings and the people they affected, and making direct amends, whether by apology, by compensation, or by prayer.

5. Community service

When you've been given the gift of forgiveness and a second chance in this world, it is crucial that you return the favor and work towards the betterment of the community. This includes attending regular meetings to keep yourself in good shape and be of support to others in the group, protesting outside vampire establishments with other Fellowship of the Sun members, cleaning up popcorn from the chapel's floor after movie night*, and signing up to be an usher during Christmas service. Those crowds can get rowdy!

**About three years ago, in an effort to attract a younger congregation, we started a film series at the church. Our membership grew over 7% the month we started it, with* The Passion of the Christ *as our grand opening. Up next?* Tim Tebow: On a Mission.

6. Devoting yourself to the cause

And what's the cause? Ridding the world of vampires, of course! It nearly destroyed your life, and you have a chance to prevent that from happening to innocent people in the future. Can you hear the flapping of angels' wings yet? I can!

Additional Tips for Recovering Fangbangers

Regular schedule: Try to get yourself on a regular schedule consisting of an early morning rise with the sun and a strict, post-sundown curfew. This will prevent unwanted vampire run-ins and help curb those nightly urges.

Diet and exercise: Eat properly and power-walk at least three times a week. Taking care of your body will help diminish cravings and remind you that God created you in the greatest image of all: His own.

Actually, we really appreciate an organic diet. It's the way nature intended blood to taste.

Therapy regimen: Join our support group, attend meetings regularly, and set up an individual therapy plan tailored to your needs.

Jettison excuses: Do not let petty things like time, access, or money prevent you from devoting yourself to your recovery. You are worth it!

Build a new life: Get more involved with the church, make new friends, and find a career with stability and structure.

WE'RE ALWAYS LOOKING FOR TALENTED DANCERS AT FANGTASIA.

Avoid triggers: Unless accompanied by a Fellowship of the Sun chaperone, steer clear of people and places from your past. They will only try to lure you back to the devil's dugout.

IN CASE OF EMERGENCY DAY-TIME LANDING

FORCED LANDING ON WATER

FORZADO ATERRIZAJE EN AGUA

FORCED LANDING ON LAND

FORZADO ATERRIZAJE EN TIERRA

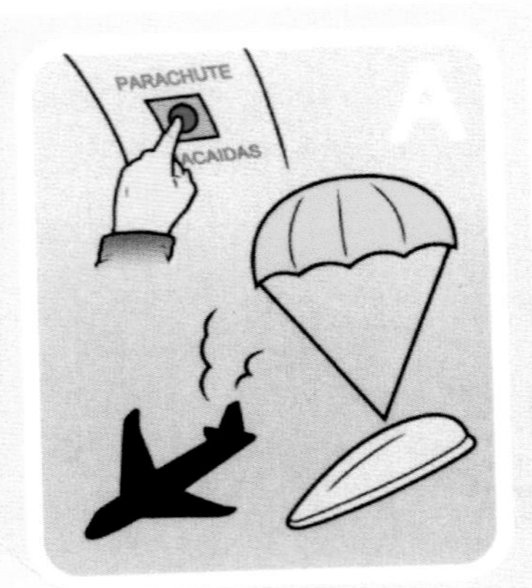

IF SAFE TO EXIT TRAVEL COFFIN, HELP YOURSELF BEFORE HELPING CHILDREN AND OTHERS.

VAMPIRE OWNED-AND-OPERATED

Since the Great Revelation, many entrepreneurs–fanged and human alike–have sought to capitalize on the newly developing vampire market. A host of novel rackets have come to the fore, some of them even garnering enough repute to join the Better Business Bureau.* Just the other day, it was brought to my attention that stores as prominent as Target and Walmart carry clothing designed by vampire reality show celebrity Babette Bailey, right alongside a line of adorable makeup created by the wholesome Christian rocker Amanda Jayne. The juxtaposition is both staggering and outrageous. A vulgar oxymoron, if you ask me! It feels like our very streets and towns are being bought up by vampires, with vampire insurance companies, light-tight curtain specialists, and vampire beauty salons on nearly every corner. How long do you think it will take Starbucks to open up Tru Blood coffee bars?†

One of the biggest and busiest vampire business sectors is the travel industry. Since vampires came out of the coffin, they've been very hungry to see the world. I'm sure they're interested in tasting humans from different places, wondering if a Louisianan or a Texan tastes any different from an Italian or a Viennese. I won't purport to know or care what human blood tastes like (unless it was Christ's, who offered wine to his disciples, saying it was his blood–I am only a vampire for Jesus!), but I will point out that we all come from a common bloodline: the Creator's.

ANUBIS AIRLINES, which opened for business just days after the Great Revelation, has all but cornered the market on vampire air travel. With a fleet of nearly two hundred planes, Anubis operates both domestically and internationally, flying vampires just about everywhere their dead hearts desire. With major hubs in Los Angeles, New York, Miami, and Houston, it's one of the fastest-growing airlines in the history of the United States. Now when vampires travel, unless traversing only very short distances, they journey in specially fabricated airtight coffins, typically provided by the airline. Although some vampires that travel on a more regular basis have opted to purchase their own travel coffins, most use the ones provided by the airlines.

* If you want to know whether a business is owned by a creature of God or by a creature of Satan, please visit us at www.fellowshipofthesun.org, and click on our "Where NOT to spend your hard-earned dollars!" link. It will provide you with all the information you'll need to properly assess a business and its vampire connections.

† Come to think of it, this is not a terrible idea for PHASE 2. If we could open a chain of Starbucks-like Tru Blood cafes, lure a trusting vampire population into our doors, and then taint the synthetic beverages with colloidal silver, we might be able to weaken the unwitting species and reclaim domination! (And get rich doing it. Maybe call it "TruBucks"?)

Even though vampires don't technically sleep, vampire hotels have become particularly popular in the last few years. Most offer a donor room service menu, where vampires can order humans exactly to their liking: fat, skinny, tall, short, even albino or freckled! And to think humans volunteer for jobs like this, happy to be products at a meat market! The rooms at these hotels are expectedly light-tight, and are often rented by the hour, which can only mean one thing: whoring. But of course the police never attempt to bust these rings, since the line between paying for blood and paying for sex has yet to be defined by our legal system. I also think cops are pansies when it comes to the illegal activities of vampires, but that's a whole other ball of un-American wax.

Back on the hotel front, the more upscale HOTEL CARMILLA in Dallas is a popular destination for vampires throughout the South, while the BLOODY BERKELEY B&B serves the Northwest with glowing reviews on VampTravel.com. There are several other inns and motels throughout the United States, with new ones popping up almost daily. The growing vampire business world suggests something very concerning to me: that the vampire population is growing too. That vampires are repeatedly kidnapping and turning humans, just another slice of their global domination pizza.

Anyhoo, in addition to travel and accommodation, vampire bars and nightclubs have quickly become a mainstay in the South. So I did a little digging and here's what I found . . .

KNOWN VAMPIRE HANGOUTS AND HOT SPOTS IN THE SOUTH

Fangtasia

Located in the shadows of Shreveport, Louisiana, this vampire-filled septic tank is owned and operated by Area 5 Sheriff Eric Northman and his consort, Pamela Swynford de Beaufort. Other employees have included their formerly undead colleagues Longshadow and Chow Lin, as well as both devoted and dimwitted fangbanger Ginger.

A filth magnet for leather-daddies and fangbangers of varying degrees, Fangtasia opened after the Great Revelation as part of the AVL's widespread mainstreaming movement. The menu offers a wide range of Tru Blood cocktails, and feeding upon humans is "forbidden," but considering this is basically the vampire Studio 54 of Louisiana, complete with human go-go dancers of both sexes twirling on slippery poles, I'm sure human blood drinking is common, if not welcomed, behind closed doors. If these walls could talk, I shudder to think what pornographic opus would unfurl.

Eric and I were briefly members at the Drake. When they first opened, we wanted to get to know our competition. Fortunately their prices have driven a large number of their clientele our way. It's a rough economy, ain't it?

The Drake

More upscale than its Shreveport counterpart, this New Orleans nightclub is modeled after the smoky speakeasies of Prohibition-era America. Patronage is exclusive to members only, with vampires allowed to join for free, while humans pay fees in excess of $3,000 a year to mingle with bloodsuckers in the world's most famous vampire location outside Transylvania. I hope they feel like they got their money's worth when they burn in hell for eternity.

Biter's

This sports bar located in Baton Rouge, Louisiana spreads its doors wide open for drunken frat boys and sorority sisters looking to catch up on the latest scores while scoring with the local vampire community. The bar is famously staffed with recently turned "baby vamps" dressed to look like all-American, fun-loving college kids, loading up their clientele with cheap shots and hurricanes before (we can assume) sucking them bone dry. Parents, this is what your hard-earned college tuition money is buying you!

IF YOU WANT TO HANG OUT WITH A BUNCH OF DRUNK MEATHEADS, NO NEED TO GO ALL THE WAY TO BATON ROUGE. MERLOTTE'S IS JUST A SHORT DRIVE AWAY.

Coffin House

This former funeral home in Birmingham, Alabama has been converted into an all-night local coffee shop open only when—you guessed it—the sun don't shine. While human insomniacs sip down their espressos, local vamps lurk over their laptops sucking down a variety of hot, coffee-inspired True Blood drinks with names like "Bloody Latte," "Capillaryccino" and "American-O Negative."

Who wants to sit around with a gaggle of sexless intellectuals anyway?

Plantation

This controversially-themed night club in Savannah, Georgia recreates a late, Southern gothic mansion, where the human waiters are dressed in servants' clothing and deliver Tru Blood cocktails to an exclusively vampire clientele. The human slavery implication is gut-wrenching and downright criminal. The Fellowship has been petitioning to shut this business down for years, but our cries of protest have fallen on the deaf, vampire-friendly ears of the local government. Perhaps an act of God, say, a fire, will do the job instead . . . ?

I keep asking Eric to take me here, but he refuses.

WHY SHOULD I SIP TRU BLOOD WITH A CROWD OF SELF-INDULGENT VAMPIRES DRESSED IN SEERSUCKER SUITS AND KENTUCKY BOW-TIES WHEN I CAN DRINK FOR FREE RIGHT HERE?

DRINK SPECIALS

FOR TEETOTALERS

Glamourade
Lime Juice, Sparkling Water, and
Housemade Blackberry Syrup

Virgin Blood
Grenadine, Cherry and Grapefruit Juices, Ginger
Ale, and Skewered Cherries

Lumière Sparklers
Ginger and Rosemary Infusion, Pomegranate Juice, and
Sparkling Apple Cider

FOR BOOZEHOUNDS

V Shooters
Whiskey, Triple Sec, Cranberry Juice, and
Berry Pulp

True Death
Tequila, Orange Juice, Grenadine, and
Crème de Cassis

No Pain No Drain
Tomato Juice, Vodka, Pickled Jalapeño Brine,
and a Savory Spice Melange

THE EMERGENCE OF ANTI-VAMPIRE SUPPLY STORES

In the wake of the Great Revelation, vampire business has not been the only growing sector in the market. Brave patriots, in an effort to arm themselves against the fanged creatures, have also begun funding a new venture: anti-vampire supplies.

Lumber companies have developed stake factories, and bullet manufacturers are flooding gun shops with thousands of new wooden and silver bullets.* There's also been a renaissance in the world of boutique weapons manufacturers, who've found success making colloidal silver misters, crossbows with wooden arrows, and even silver nail polish! Wouldn't you just love to paint that on and dig your fingernails into a nasty vampire? We all have our fantasies, I suppose, I just never expected mine to involve nail lacquer! *Plenty of mine involve nail lacquer. And hot wax. And underaged coeds.*

Not only are the manufacturers taking advantage of this new demand, but plenty of Americans with enough capital and enough common decency are opening stores solely devoted to the sale of these weapons. Here are a few with my very own stamp of approval:

* I was even asked to participate in an ad campaign for vampire hunting gear . . . And for a small price, I was thrilled to oblige. The split with Sarah is draining my bank account like a rent-a-boy in a vampire orgy!

The Stake House

The Stake House, which recently opened in Forbing, Louisiana, just outside of Shreveport, was one of the first of its kind and has seen steady business. The shop, helmed by Junior Boggs III, began as a mail-order service in the garage of Junior's studio apartment just days after the Great Revelation. It advertised "vamp defense equipment," and mostly offered homemade stakes and silver chain link. After saving enough money, Junior managed to parlay his small mail-order business into a brick-and-mortar operation, carrying over one hundred varying forms of anti-vamp devices and weaponry. Junior is a big fan of mine and an all-around good guy.

They say you can attract more flies with honey, but sometimes flies just like the smell of shit. This particular fly is no more; he was part of a hate group called the Obamas and was killed by Sam Merlotte.

Vamp Off

Since the Stake House's success, several similar stores have opened. Vamp Off was one of the first to follow suit, breaking ground in Morgan City and earning a huge clientele, mostly by word of mouth.

Silverado's

Alexandria's anti-vamp emporium is by far the largest in Louisiana. They've got great prices and great products. If you're buying in bulk, this is the place to go!

These idiots can't even get their facts straight. Everyone knows that vampires turn to goo, not dust, when they meet the True Death.

Vamps "R" Dust

Now I've visited quite a few of these joints, and this is by far my favorite. Maybe it's because it's in Beaumont, and I'm partial to Texas. But I think it's because the owner has an arsenal that could rival my own, and I'm a gun enthusiast, what can I say! And to make the deal even sweeter, the employees started a newsletter that tracks all known vampires in the great Lone Star state. Publicly, they claim it's simply for preventative safety, kind of like Megan's Law, but they admitted to me that the gather this information to help plan their vamp hunts . . .

WSDS: WEAPONS OF SATANIC DESTRUCTION

Sounds to me like Newlin has a real obsession with phallic symbols.

We cannot ignore this myriad of findings. The threat of the supernatural is at our very doorstep.* We can invite it into our homes, dance with the devil, and sell our souls, or we can arm ourselves, fight back, and stand up for God. We can make sure brave warriors like my father did not die in vain, but for a cause greater than all of us.

Once PHASE 2 commences, and we spread the word about Satan and his militiamen, I have no doubt we will find ourselves in the midst of World War III: Armageddon. This is a battle we can win using two crucial tools: prayer and weaponry. I have my suspicions that the U.S. government is developing advanced artillery to combat vampires, but in case this turns out to be false, we need backup. So I am taking matters into my own hands! I recently enlisted a team of engineers to manufacture state-of-the-art armaments. Here are a few of the ideas we're working on so far:

VAMP DUSTERS: Modified crop dusters that will spray colloidal silver mist over known vampire nests and hangouts. These puppies are so stealthy that even vamp hearing won't detect them until they're just a football field away!

CRISPERS: These bad boys are retrofitted bazookas and rocket pods that not only launch silver-dipped rocket-propelled missiles, but double as flamethrowers! We're trying to see if they can also shoot streams of pure liquefied silver, but the precious metal needs to be kept at over 1,600 degrees Fahrenheit and we've been having trouble maintaining temperatures in our lab tests . . . nothing that can't be solved with a little elbow grease and some well-mannered pleas to God!

LITTLE DARLINS: Standard combat pistols made of silver, so if a vampire overtakes the holder, he can't use it against us! And get this: they're designed specifically to shoot wooden bullets up to 3,000 FPS!†

Even with these weapons, this will not be an easy crusade. But with Jesus as our general, there is nothing we cannot achieve.

There is, however, another tactic we can use to our advantage, that has little to do with God or guns . . . STRENGTH IN NUMBERS. There's more of us than there are of them. It's simple playground arithmetic. If our boys and our men line up and sign up, and our women man the factories and hospitals in their absence, we can nip Armageddon in the bud and get on with enjoying God's green earth.

* I am speaking both literally and figuratively here. For the last few weeks, I swear I can hear the clicks of fangs and the whooshes of vampires coming and going from the grounds outside my hotel room (much to my dismay, it looks like Sarah's getting the house in the divorce). I fear I am being watched, plotted against, perhaps to be the next victim of Satan's army. I have just assigned one of my best Soldiers of the Sun squads to be my own personal security detail, but I still fear for my life. Hopefully I'm just being paranoid, and it's only Sarah's private investigator snooping around for dirt on me that he'll never find. You can't find what doesn't exist, am I right?

† FPS, which stands for feet per second, is the stand measurement of bullet speed. While 3,000 FPS isn't an outrageous speed for the more commonly found lead bullets, we're wading into new territory here with wooden bullets. I'm shooting for the moon–I've got my heart set on a Guinness Book of World Records entry!

SOLDIERS OF THE SUN
BITE BACK!
L.O.D.I.
FIGHT FOR YOUR FREEDOM FROM FANGS

VAMPIRES: THE FIRST WAVE OF THE APOCALYPSE

My father was certainly correct when he said that "we live in exciting times." But he left out one word: terrifying. The war against evil has begun, with vampires forming the frontline of Satan's army. They will act swiftly to wipe out humanity the moment we let down our guard and allow them into our homes, schools, government, and bedrooms. The time to man up is now.

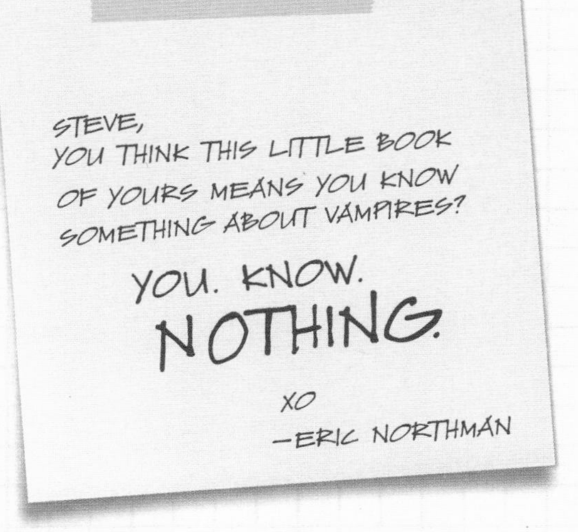

OTHER CREATURES OF SATAN

As it turns out, the Great Revelation wasn't really that great. We only found out about vampires. However, they are just the tip of the supernatural iceberg. There is in fact a myriad of ungodly creatures that have walked amongst us for centuries. It's a hard truth, but one we must accept:
SATAN HAS REINFORCEMENTS!

A BRIEF INTRODUCTION

If the dog is considered to be man's best friend, then I'd consider the werewolf to be Satan's bitch. Where vampires crave the blood of humans, werewolves hunger for only one thing: the sweet, savory taste of human flesh. While not as powerful as vampires, werewolves are extremely private supernatural pack animals who can quickly overrun a large community of humans. Their ferocity and strength is not to be underestimated and their loyalty to their dark master is unwavering.

History and Lore

When I was a tyke, I always got scared during the full moon. Unbeknownst to my father, I had seen a scary movie during a sleepover at a friend's house that introduced me to the horror of werewolves and led to countless nightmares of being chased by slavering, panting beasts looking to snack on little Stevie. The movie was a haunting tale about a high school basketball player who turned into a wolfman during the full moon, going on to terrorize his fellow students while getting drunk at parties and doing headstands on moving vehicles. I couldn't sleep for weeks after seeing that film!

Turns out, my fears weren't unfounded, even if the movie didn't really get all the facts straight. Werewolves do exist. And after vampires, they are humanity's second largest supernatural threat. Like vamps, they have been hunting down humans for centuries; the earliest accounts of werewolf sightings date back to 12th century France and Germany. The wolf bloodline may trace all the way back to Heinrich IX, the Black Duke of Bavaria and member of the European dynasty, the House Welf (or "Wolf"). The name says it all. Heinrich was known for his violent nature, and some tales suggested he had the ability to change into a wolf and run wild (perhaps given lycanthropic powers by Satan in exchange for servitude?). Was Heinrich the first werewolf? I doubt it. After all, in that movie about the teenage werewolf, the men in his family had been werewolves for generations. Who knows how far back into history werewolves go? Unfortunately, the longer they remain hidden from the public, the less we'll know about their secrets.

I've yet to meet a MEMORABLE werewolf, let alone one you could call "legendary."

Legendary Wolves

<u>THE WOLVES OF PARIS:</u>
In French folklore, the werewolf is commonly referred to as <u>loup-garou</u>, a term that is sometimes used here in the South, having been brought over by our French and Creole ancestors. During the winter of 1450, a pack of man-eating werewolves terrorized the city of Paris, killing dozens of humans, before finally being rounded up and stoned to death by a large militia of humans outside Notre Dame cathedral. See what can happen when you have God on your side?

<u>THE BEAST OF GEVAUDAN:</u>
Actually, there was more than one beast in this legend, as at least two werewolves were said to have hunted French villagers in the province of Gevaudan during the mid-1760s. This account marks the first recorded use of a silver bullet to kill a monster-an important moment in the war against supes!

<u>THE GHOST PACK:</u> *MET THEM. DESTROYED THEM.*
I've heard whispers of a nomadic pack of werewolves responsible for a number of ghost towns spread throughout the United States. This pack, noted for the skull-like markings on their faces, worships a werewolf deity named "Croatoan." They may be native to this continent, and are possibly responsible for the disappearance of the Roanoke colony, whose inhabitants mysteriously disappeared overnight. The word "Croatoan" was etched into a tree, perhaps warning other colonists that those lands belonged to someone else.

A DISCOVERY OF WOLVES

I first discovered the furry friend (and often foe) of vampires-the werewolf-during a search-and-destroy mission by my elite squad of the Soldiers of the Sun. This was shortly after "The Incident." Sarah and I were fighting, I had been emasculated in front of my followers by Eric Northman and Bill Compton, so I decided to up my game and make a preemptive strike against a vampire known as Curly who was living in a hippie compound outside Austin, Texas.

I sent a few of my best men down to the compound during the day (always best to slay a fanger in their sleep-lessens the risk), armed with stakes. We expected a few devoted humans to be guarding Curly's coffin, but my men were shocked to find that the place was relatively empty, aside from three women asleep in ground floor rooms. Well, let me tell you, these gals were certainly devoted to Curly, but they were definitely not human.

Those harpies shifted into wolves right in front of my men. Shots were fired, teeth gnashed, blood splattered the walls. When all was said and done, only one of my men made it back to me, and he died in my arms uttering "Those eyes . . . those horrible orange eyes!" Needless to say, I was in total shock.

I went online to gather as much information about werewolves as I could. One of the first things that popped up was Operation Werwolf, which was associated with this "Wolfsangel," a German word for "wolf's hook," represented by a symbol that looked almost like an unfinished swastika.

According to my findings, this was an actual plan set forth by the Nazis during World War II to infiltrate Allied Forces using an elite command squad. Of course, the "werewolf" was generally assumed to be a metaphor, and this was thought to be just a human-run operation (after all, this is decades before vampires came out of the coffin, a time when monsters were socially accepted as imaginary), but as I dug a little deeper, I found more and more eyewitness accounts of actual werewolves fighting for the Nazis during WWII!

AHH, BRINGS BACK THE GOOD OLD DAYS WITH GODRIC.

Indeed, truth is stranger than fiction, as I've learned of a related branch of Wolfsangel-branded wolves working under the employ of Russell Edgington, the vampire king of Mississippi. I have linked this pack to a few known wolves: a male by the name of Cooter*, his female companion Deborah Pelt, and a rather beefy fellow by the name of Alcide Herveaux. It appears to be that Alcide is a good friend of–you guessed it–Sookie Stackhouse, but I have yet to figure out how or why. I know for a fact that Sookie is not a werewolf, so why the fraternizing? Does she just sleep around with everything that moves? I'm somewhat inclined to believe it is just her trampy nature that keeps her engaged with so many supernaturals. Or perhaps it is part of some larger plan to unite supernaturals against humans? We'll have to wait and see.

* I once had an Uncle Cooter. He wasn't my real uncle, but he was my father's college roommate and he sort of filled that space in my life for a time. He taught me how to throw a baseball when my dad was too busy, and he bought me my first beer the day I turned twenty-one. He was later arrested for public indecency (turns out he was flashing coeds behind the Dumpster of a local sorority house) and my father broke off communication with him. I still receive letters from Uncle Coot in prison from time to time, but I'm afraid his actions forever tainted the phrase "Let's play ball."

THE ABILITIES AND POWERS OF WEREWOLVES

* WEREWOLVES ARE TWO-NATURED CREATURES, meaning they have two forms of appearance-human and wolf-with the ability to shift freely between the two at will.

* The only time a werewolf cannot shift at will or revert to human form is during THE LIGHT OF THE FULL MOON.

* Werewolves have advanced strength and agility, even in human form. Though generally, they are weaker than vampires.

* Werewolves possess HEIGHTENED SENSES in both human and wolf form. They have keen senses of smell, sight, and hearing, which make them exceptional hunters and give them an advantage over humans.

* Apparently, a human cannot be made into a werewolf by being bitten, despite what we've seen in countless Hollywood movies. WEREWOLVES MUST BE BORNE OF ONE OR TWO WEREWOLF PARENTS. If there is only one werewolf parent, there is a 50/50 chance the child will remain human, but two werewolf parents will produce a werewolf cub 100 percent of the time.*

* Werewolves can be detected by their GLOWING ORANGE OR AMBER EYES, which appear when angered or in wolf form. If you see those eyes light up, it's time to skedaddle!

* I thought Sarah liked her meat raw (she orders it medium rare, hello!), but it turns out these swine have her beat. When in wolf form, they eat their meat completely uncooked. I wonder if they've ever been plagued with E. coli?

YOU FORGOT TO MENTION THEIR BAD BREATH.

It should be noted that vampires have gotten away with victimizing humans for so long because they have the ability to glamour; they can simply erase the memory of interactions from humans' minds. Werewolves, however, cannot glamour their victims, so instead they make sure very few, if any, walk away alive. But the lucky ones that do evade their grasp? They remember every horrible moment of their attack.

* I must admit, I find it rather unsettling to think that a human-a creature of God-can actually give birth to a werewolf if implanted with the seed of a werewolf mate. It seems to go against the very nature of humanity. But then again, I've seen the trailer for Rosemary's Baby, so I suppose we're all susceptible to being impregnated by the devil himself!

PACK ANIMALS

Werewolves are pack animals. It is in their very nature to surround themselves with their own kind, and it is extremely rare for them to be seen with less than three or four other wolves.

I have encountered a handful of packs in my studies, and while they are each different from one another, they share some commonalities. All packs have a leader, or "packmaster." Wolves crave structure and guidance. Without an alpha to run the show, packs will dissolve into utter chaos. And while the majority of packs exhibit the utmost loyalty and dedication, many are tainted by inner turmoil and bitter politics. Packmaster is a coveted position, one that can only be seized upon the death or disappearance of the current packmaster. Some packs wait for a natural death to occur, while others opt for mutiny, in which one male member kills or runs off the reigning alpha.* This makes for a very tumultuous and tentative rule, resulting in paranoid packmasters constantly looking over their shoulders. The truth is, the role proves to be too burdensome for many, and as a consequence, packs often witness a changing of the guard.

Boys will be boys.

But packs aren't just full of testosterone-filled man-beasts. There are also female wolves, known as "bitches," who, incidentally, also seem to be filled with testosterone. I don't think I've ever seen such rough-and-tumble women in my life, and I've watched the LPGA! And, of course, let's not forget the children: pups. Baby wolves run with their parents' pack, and upon approaching puberty, are initiated as official members. The initiation typically comes in the form of a ceremony, but the rituals vary from pack to pack. Some involve hunting, some involve drinking the blood of dead animals, and some necessitate a lot of ancient, puffed-up language.

* I have to admit, this reminds me a bit of my fraternity days, when a handful of my brothers ousted our president Ronny Muckes (pronounced like mucus, poor kid!) because his father, who happened to be president of the university, was indicted on charges of fraud. The boys didn't want to risk dragging our house's name through the mud, so they put all of his furniture and belongings on the front lawn and had the place rekeyed. He got the hint and resigned immediately, never to be seen on campus again.

TERRITORY

It is rare to find more than one pack living in a given area, as werewolves are also highly territorial. They view their land as hunting grounds belonging to their pack, and their pack alone. Infringement upon their hallowed ground is seen as an act of war, so most packs are respectful and understanding of this arrangement. I've managed to put together a map of known werewolf packs in the South, but given the private nature of werewolves, I fear it is a template at best.

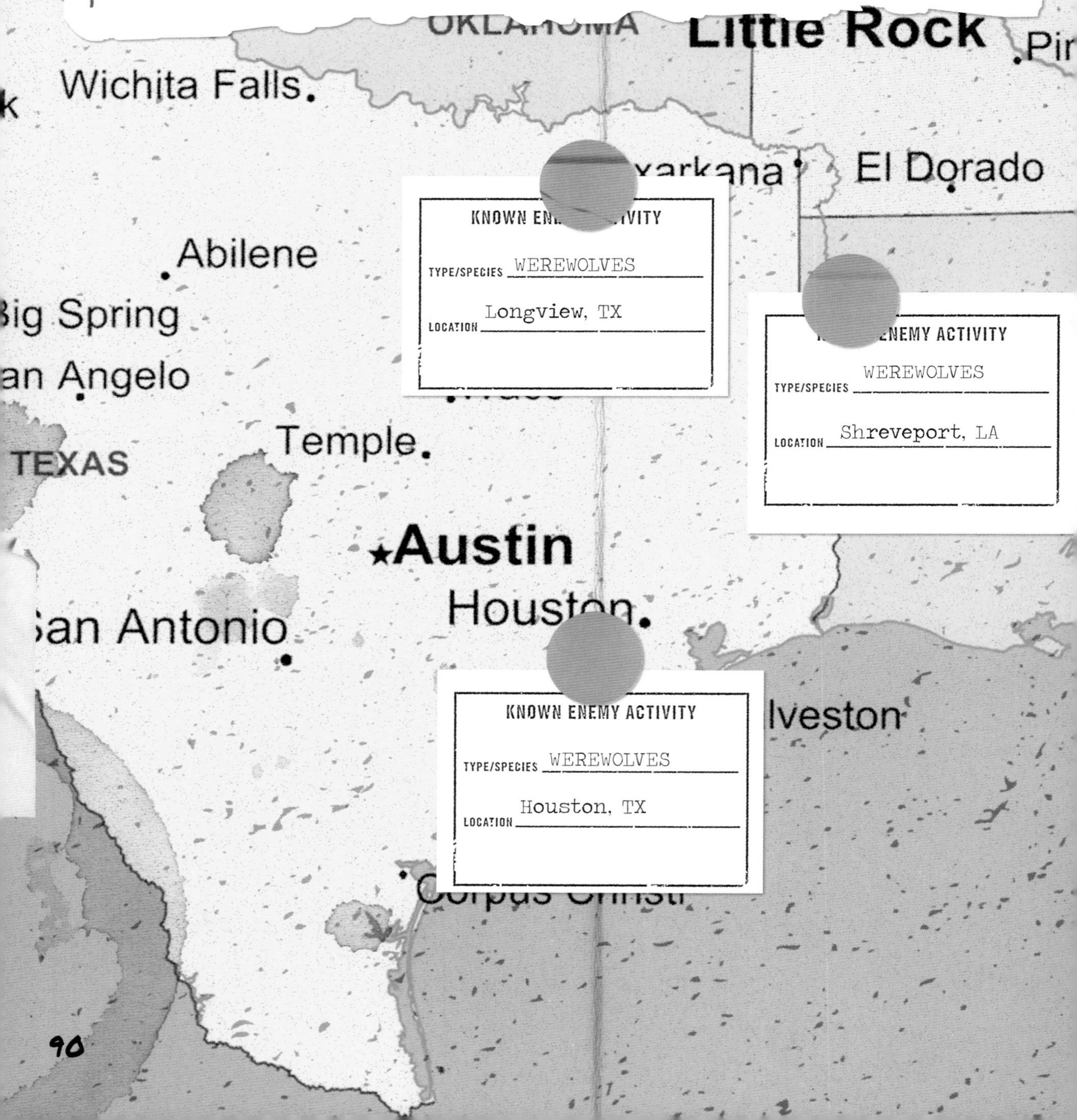

KNOWN EN… …IVITY

TYPE/SPECIES: WEREWOLVES

LOCATION: Longview, TX

…ENEMY ACTIVITY

TYPE/SPECIES: WEREWOLVES

LOCATION: Shreveport, LA

KNOWN ENEMY ACTIVITY

TYPE/SPECIES: WEREWOLVES

LOCATION: Houston, TX

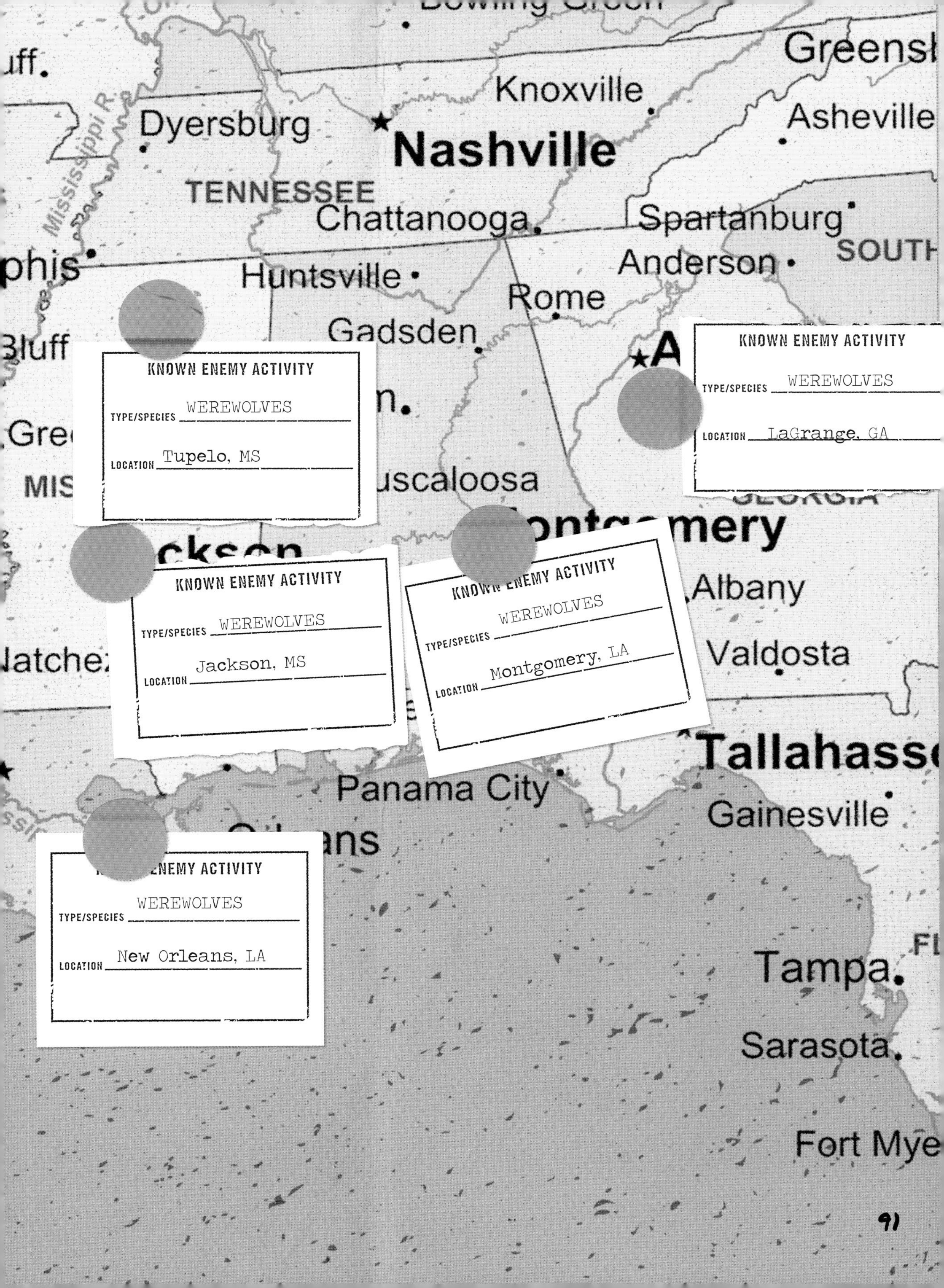
KNOWN ENEMY ACTIVITY
TYPE/SPECIES WEREWOLVES
LOCATION Tupelo, MS
KNOWN ENEMY ACTIVITY
TYPE/SPECIES WEREWOLVES
LOCATION LaGrange, GA
KNOWN ENEMY ACTIVITY
TYPE/SPECIES WEREWOLVES
LOCATION Jackson, MS
KNOWN ENEMY ACTIVITY
TYPE/SPECIES WEREWOLVES
LOCATION Montgomery, LA
ENEMY ACTIVITY
TYPE/SPECIES WEREWOLVES
LOCATION New Orleans, LA
Knoxville
Asheville
Dyersburg
Nashville
TENNESSEE
Chattanooga
Spartanburg
Anderson
Huntsville
Rome
Gadsden
Albany
Valdosta
Tallahassee
Panama City
Gainesville
Tampa
Sarasota

LOU PINE'S

November 29

Despite their highly secretive nature, I managed to track several werewolves-mostly from the Jackson pack-to one location: Lou Pine's. It appears to be a werewolf bar near Battlefield Park in Jackson, Mississippi. The door is heavily guarded by bouncer Hollis Ardoin, a werewolf the size of at least three Dallas Cowboys linebackers, combined. He seems to operate under the instructions that if you're not a wolf, you're not getting into the joint.

In addition to their privacy, they clearly like their puns. Lou Pine's is a play on the word lupine, which refers to anything characteristic of or relating to a wolf. It comes from the Latin name for wolf: canis lupus. I'd like to open a can of lupus on those werewolves!* Get it? Nah, I'm not sure that one really works . . .

I'm positive it doesn't.

* I'm compiling all the comebacks to supernatural creatures I can think of. So far my favorites are: Read it and weep blood tears and Hasta la vista, baby vamp!

HOLLIS ARDOIN

Bouncer & Private Security

Lou
PINE'S
BEER

KNOWN ENEMY

NAME Alcide Herveaux

SPECIES Werewolf

STATUS Active

PACK Formerly Jackson, Mississippi, ~~currently not affiliated~~

KNOWN RELATIVES Father Jackson Herveaux (an ex-packmaster), sister Janice Herveaux (hairdresser and fashion stylist)

OCCUPATION Contractor

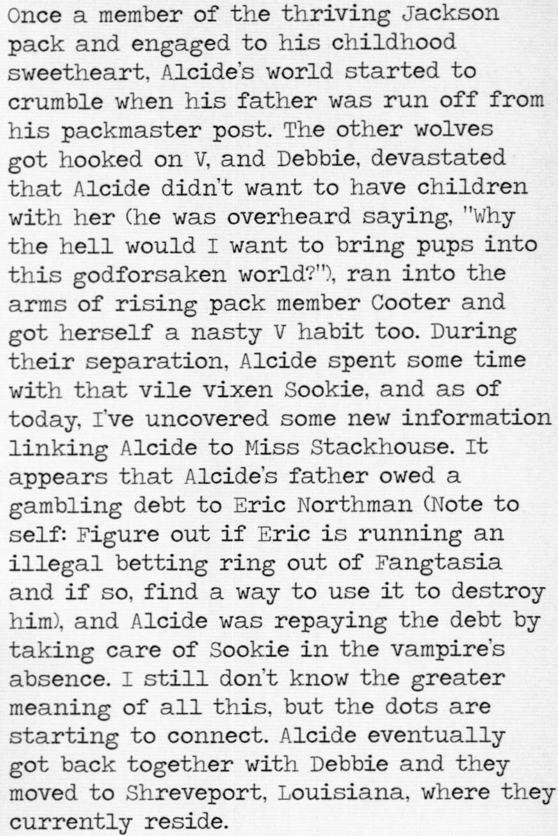

Once a member of the thriving Jackson pack and engaged to his childhood sweetheart, Alcide's world started to crumble when his father was run off from his packmaster post. The other wolves got hooked on V, and Debbie, devastated that Alcide didn't want to have children with her (he was overheard saying, "Why the hell would I want to bring pups into this godforsaken world?"), ran into the arms of rising pack member Cooter and got herself a nasty V habit too. During their separation, Alcide spent some time with that vile vixen Sookie, and as of today, I've uncovered some new information linking Alcide to Miss Stackhouse. It appears that Alcide's father owed a gambling debt to Eric Northman (Note to self: Figure out if Eric is running an illegal betting ring out of Fangtasia and if so, find a way to use it to destroy him), and Alcide was repaying the debt by taking care of Sookie in the vampire's absence. I still don't know the greater meaning of all this, but the dots are starting to connect. Alcide eventually got back together with Debbie and they moved to Shreveport, Louisiana, where they currently reside.

Probably on his way to becoming packmaster, considering how he swings his dick around like he owns the whole town.

KNOWN ENEMY

NAME Debbie Pelt

SPECIES Werewolf

STATUS ~~Active~~ *Ding dong, the bitch is dead!*

PACK Formerly Jackson, Mississippi, currently not affiliated

KNOWN RELATIVES Mother Barbara Pelt, father Gordon Pelt

OCCUPATION Homemaker

NOTES

Having grown up in the Jackson pack of werewolves, Debbie fell in love with Alcide at a very young age. But like Alcide, Debbie had her own family struggles. Her mother suffered a somewhat lengthy bout with alcoholism, and her father had a temper that could rival Sarah's*. After taking V for the first time, Debbie was never the same. She destroyed her life with Alcide in favor of regular V binges and the company of a gang of biker werewolves. Debbie eventually cleaned up her act, found Jesus, and convinced Alcide to give things another try. After a year now, she appears to be sober, attends regular support group meetings, and keeps a lovely home. For a wolf, of course. Despite her desperation to join the local Shreveport pack, her pleas have fallen on deaf ears; Alcide has no desire to be anything but what he describes as a "free agent."

* Very few people know this, but Sarah actually suffered terrible fits of rage as a child, and was consequently put into anger management therapy. A woman named Lisa would come over to her home to "play games" with her, observe how Sarah would react to losing Sorry! or Parcheesi, and work with her to manage her temper tantrums. Sarah eventually learned to cope with her abnormal anger, but every now and again, the beast would come out-and it was <u>not</u> pretty!

KNOWN ENEMY

NAME Martha Bozeman

SPECIES Werewolf

STATUS Active

PACK Shreveport

KNOWN RELATIVES Son Marcus Bozeman, granddaughter Emma Garza

OCCUPATION Unknown (she seems a little too gruff to be a homemaker!)

NOTES

Once married to the Shreveport packmaster and father of Marcus, Martha's world was turned upside down when her husband died young and her son took over the pack. Despite her differences with many of the Shreveport wolves, Martha remains one of the most feared and revered members of this pack.

KNOWN ENEMY

NAME Marcus Bozeman

SPECIES Werewolf

STATUS Active

PACK Shreveport

KNOWN RELATIVES Mother Martha Bozeman, daughter Emma Garza

OCCUPATION Packmaster/Motorcycle shop owner

NOTES

A recovering addict who struggles with intermittent relapses, Marcus is the fearless leader of the Shreveport pack. He runs a motorcycle shop he opened with money from his father's life insurance policy and tends to any and all pack matters when not working on his bikes. Despite being well-respected by his peers, he has a tendency to stick his things in other people's business . . . mainly wives and girlfriends.

KNOWN ENEMY

NAME Cooter *a.k.a. "Coot," also the name of my favorite pastime.*

SPECIES Werewolf

STATUS Deceased

PACK Jackson, Mississippi

KNOWN RELATIVES None

OCCUPATION Head of the Fuck You Crew

NOTES

The leader of a werewolf biker gang best known as the Fuck You Crew, Cooter was a repugnant V junkie with a penchant for violence and sleeping with other wolves' women. He and his cronies worked for Russell Edgington in exchange for an endless supply of the vampire king's blood.

WERE ELSE?

As if werewolves weren't bad enough, the buck don't stop there. Because Satan isn't satisfied to have just one pet, there's a whole assortment of were-creatures running around out there. In fact, I think this town Jason's been visiting so often, Hot Shot, is actually inhabited by a bunch of backwoods werepanthers. This could explain a rash of mysterious giant black cat sightings that have plagued the South for decades, long after the last of the North American panthers were killed off. I don't know much about this little number, Crystal, who's been involved with Jason lately, but I do know that her trash couldn't get any whiter. Let's pray he gets over her quickly. I mean, not that I care about his feelings or anything, I just don't want anyone getting to him before I do. If anyone is gonna sink their claws into Jason Stackhouse, it's going to be me!

AT LEAST HE'S MOVED UP FROM THIS KIND OF TRASH TO VAMPIRES; HE'S CURRENTLY INVOLVED WITH JESSICA HAMBY. BUT YOU'RE ALLOWED TO DREAM ABOUT HIM ALL YOU WANT, STEVE . . .

So if there are werewolves and werepanthers out there . . . what else? Werebears? Perhaps even weretigers? Furthermore, I'm uncovering that there are even weres that can shift into any animal they fancy. Wouldn't they be the shiftiest shifters of all?

How I feel about werewolves, werepanthers, or any other weres for that matter, is not much of a secret in my circle of vampires. I can't fucking stand them, to put it lightly. They're pitilessly developmentally challenged, they smell like mangy pieces of fecal matter, and furthermore, they're uppity enough to think they can hang with the likes of vampires. They bicker amongst themselves like bratty schoolchildren about who is the stronger, faster, better were, but the reality is that they're all inferior species.

Look at those toothless fucktards from Hot Shot. Now I know a thing or two about pushing drugs, thanks to my colorful past. And the most important thing about making a sale? Don't use up your entire stash before it even hits the market. Those meth-dealers-turned-meth-heads are only capable of two things: beating the shit out of each other over trashy girls and misunderstandings, and kidnapping Jason Stackhouse (which isn't saying much–that boy couldn't find his own ass with two hands). Meanwhile, these house cats actually believe they're sent from the heavens. They have a whole "Ghost Daddy" God saga they narrate to their children, in the hopes of instilling in them a sense of purpose. If I were the one telling tales at that campfire, I'd say this: **your purpose in life is to be less than mediocre drug dealers, less than mediocre supernatural creatures, and less than mediocre in the good looks department. Now eat your damn s'mores.**

And werewolves? They ain't much better. They're whiny dogs so unaware of their inferiority that they have actually tried to form alliances with vampires under the ruse that we're equal creatures. The next time I see that turd Alcide Herveaux, I'm going to punch him in the face so hard it sends him through the earth's core and all the way to China. Hopefully Eric won't be around, because I can just hear him now . . . As your maker, I command you not to punch that fucker. He ruins all the fun.

AU CONTRAIRE, I'M ALWAYS THE LIFE OF THE PARTY.

I pride myself in always being good, but there have been a few times I've wandered off the true path and set foot in the brambles. One of those times involved–I hate to admit it–drugs. However, in retrospect, I actually believe my experimentation was part of a larger plan by God to clue me in to the shady dealings of the diablo.

The Light of Day Institute takes all kinds. There's nothing I enjoy more than recovering a lost sheep and putting him back into God's green pastures with all the other little sheep. Our campers come from many walks of life. Sure, the majority come from fortunate homes, traditional American families that are simply concerned with the way this world is going, but Sarah and I have rescued orphans, runaways, former fangbangers, prostitutes, a transsexual, and drug addicts.

During one of our routine cabin sweeps one summer, my assistant, Gabe, may he rest in peace, came across a bag full of "Mary Jane" in a female camper's backpack. The "weed" was promptly confiscated and the camper was sent home to her parents, with permission to come back to camp once she had been properly rehabilitated through our church counseling.*

What I didn't know right away was that Sarah had brought the marijuana cigarette back to the house. After a bottle of wine and a bowl of her yummy vanilla pudding, she pulled out the "number" and talked me into smoking it. I'm ashamed to admit it, but Sarah and I had been having some problems connecting in the bedroom that July (it was just so hot, I didn't feel like having her on top of me). Sarah had experimented with "grass" back in college a couple times, and she said she had read that it could do wonders for couples

* We have a very strict zero tolerance policy at camp. While we hate to punish anyone, since God does His own punishing, we find it a necessary precaution to prevent the corruption of other more innocent campers.

looking to spice things up a little bit. Well, maybe it was the wine, or maybe it was all that sugar in my system, but I went for it. She "passed" and I reluctantly "puffed."

Sarah and I took two "hits" of the "herb" and sat back to enjoy the show. I can't say we exactly attacked one another, but things were off to a pretty good start, with some light cuddling and a strong case of the giggles. We were lying on the dining room floor, talking about the first time we met at an ice cream social, which led Sarah to suggest we make some Smackalicious Sundaes* . Never hearing a better idea in my blessed life, I happily leapt to my feet and headed for the freezer.

I stumbled into the kitchen, where Marina, our maid, had just finished the dishes. She looked at me sheepishly and informed me that she was quitting. I told her she couldn't quit, because I suddenly realized I was craving her homemade chile con queso. When I returned with Sarah from the other room to settle the matter, we discovered, much to our surprise, that Marina had disappeared-seemingly into thin air-and left her maid's uniform on the floor.

At first, I thought the Rapture was happening. But then I realized that it couldn't have possibly happened because Sarah and I were still standing in our kitchen, and not up in heaven. We slowly approached the heap of clothes, examining closely for traces of smoke or lingering electrical current from God's almighty power, when a little MOUSE came scurrying out from beneath the pile, across the floor, and through the gap under the door leading to the garage!

We were stunned. I had never seen what I have since come to know as a shapeshifter, or more simply, a SHIFTER, in action. Sarah and I thought it was the "grass" and promptly burned the clothing in a metal drum in the garage and checked all the mousetraps before retiring upstairs. We never spoke of it again, for fear that we'd be found out, or worse-sent to the nuthouse. Consequently, we gave up on fixing our sex life that night too.

Shifters live amongst us in secret, with the ability to transform themselves into any animal of their choosing (within certain limits, I'm just starting to understand). This ability makes them perfect spies for Satan. Clearly, Marina had been sent to gather information on the Fellowship of the Sun. We haven't seen hide nor hair of her since. I can only imagine what she's up to these days, and if she still makes that chile con queso.

Probably thanking her lucky stars she no longer works for you.

* These are far more addictive than "reefer" or V or any other drug for that matter. You take three scoops of chocolate ice cream, cover them in melted peanut butter, drizzle some maple syrup and toasted almonds all over, and then sprinkle rainbow jimmies on top. It is truly one of God's great gifts. Yummo!

THE NATURE OF SHIFTERS

STEVE WAS CLEARLY ONTO SOMETHING WITH HIS LITTLE "MAID THAT WAS A MOUSE" TALE, BUT THAT SEEMS TO BE THE EXTENT OF HIS SHIFTER KNOWLEDGE. SO I THOUGHT I'D HELP HIM OUT AND FILL IN A FEW BLANKS. VAMPIRES, HAVING ROAMED THE EARTH FOR LONG ENOUGH TO WITNESS THE MOST FUCKED-UP OF SUPERNATURAL FEATS, HAVE A VAST UNDERSTANDING OF THESE SHIFTY CREATURES. HERE ARE THE FACTS, COBBLED TOGETHER BY ME AND MY FAVORITE PROGENY PAM. TRUTH IS, WHEN IT COMES TO SHIFTERS, THERE ISN'T MUCH TO 'EM.

SHIFTERS SUPERNATURAL CREATURES THAT CAN TRANSFORM THEMSELVES INTO ANY ANIMAL THEY'VE **IMPRINTED** UPON.

IMPRINTING THE ACT OF OBSERVING AN ANIMAL, WHETHER LIVE OR IN A PHOTOGRAPH, AND MAKING AN INDELIBLE MENTAL IMPRESSION.

GO-TO SHIFT A SHIFTER'S DEFAULT ANIMAL, THE ONE HE CHOOSES TO TURN INTO THE MAJORITY OF THE TIME OR WHEN HE SHIFTS INVOLUNTARILY. SAM MERLOTTE'S GO-TO SHIFT IS A DOG. NOT ENTIRELY . . . CREATIVE.

THE FIRST SHIFT SHIFTERS TYPICALLY EXPERIENCE THEIR FIRST SHIFT AROUND PUBERTY. FOR SOME, LIKE PAM AND THE SIZE-D BREASTS SHE ACQUIRED BY AGE 10, IT HAPPENS EARLY. FOR OTHERS, THOSE UNFORTUNATE ACNE-RIDDEN ADOLESCENTS, THIS OCCURS IN THEIR MID-TEENS.

THE TROUBLE WITH SLEEP SHIFTERS CAN SHIFT AT WILL DURING THEIR WAKING HOURS, BUT CANNOT CONTROL SHIFTING BACK INTO THEIR HUMAN FORM WHEN THEY FALL ASLEEP.

THE TROUBLE WITH FULL MOONS LIKE WERES, SHIFTERS INVOLUNTARILY SHIFT DURING A FULL MOON.

THE TROUBLE WITH MAENADS DIONYSUS' FEMALE GROUPIES SEEM TO HAVE A PARTICULAR INTEREST IN SHIFTERS. MARYANN, THE MAENAD THAT HASSLED BON TEMPS, EXHIBITED A VIBRATING POWER THAT SEEMED TO FORCE SHIFTERS TO SHIFT.

CREATION MYTH JUST LIKE WERES, SHIFTERS CANNOT BE "TURNED" OR "MADE." THEY ARE CREATED THE OLD-FASHIONED WAY: THROUGH SEXUAL INTERCOURSE. SHIFTERS MUST BE BORNE OF AT LEAST ONE SHIFTER PARENT.

SKINWALKING ORIGINS OF SKINWALKING TRACE BACK TO NAVAJO LEGEND AND DICTATE THAT A HUMAN CAN ONLY ACQUIRE THE SUPERNATURAL POWER OF SHIFTING INTO ANOTHER HUMAN BEING BY MURDERING A MEMBER OF HIS OR HER OWN FAMILY. THE MYTHOLOGY ALSO SUGGESTS THAT A SKINWALKER, UPON TAKING OVER THE BODY OF SOMEONE ELSE, HAS ACCESS TO THE VOICE AND/OR SOUNDS OF WHATEVER "SKIN" THEY ARE IN. ALTHOUGH IT WAS TYPICALLY DISMISSED AS SILLY FOLKLORE, EVEN WITHIN THE VAMPIRE COMMUNITY, IT'S COME TO OUR ATTENTION RECENTLY THAT SKINWALKING IS ABSOLUTELY FACTUAL.

THE LOCAL SHIFTER COMMUNITY

A LOCAL SHIFTER COMMUNITY HAS RECENTLY COME TO MY ATTENTION, AND WHILE HUMANS ARE STILL UNENLIGHTENED ABOUT THESE MATTERS, VAMPIRES HAVE CAUGHT WIND OF THE SPECIES' NEW NEED TO GATHER. IN FACT, WE HAVE OUR VERY OWN LITTLE "SUPPORT GROUP" OF SHIFTERS RIGHT HERE IN BON TEMPS. SAM MERLOTTE, LUNA GARZA, AND THEIR NOW-DECEASED FRIENDS SUZANNE AND EMORY HAVE BEEN MEETING UP ONCE A MONTH TO EAT MIDDLING WHEELS OF CAMEMBERT, DRINK $9 BOTTLES OF ZINFANDEL, AND GO "RUNNING" TOGETHER (WHICH ESSENTIALLY MEANS STRIPPING DOWN TO THEIR BIRTHDAY SUITS AND ROAMING THE BACKWOODS OF LOUISIANA AS HORSES, SHEEP, DOGS, AND SQUIRRELS).

THIS KIND OF SHIFTER ORGANIZING IS A RATHER NEW OCCURRENCE, SOMETHING I'VE ONLY SEEN HAPPEN SINCE VAMPIRE MAINSTREAMING STRUCK A CHORD WITH THE CURRENT ZEITGEIST. PERHAPS THEY'VE TAKEN A PAGE FROM VAMPIRES AND STARTED TO FEEL COMFORTABLE IN THEIR OWN SKIN. BUT AS TO WHAT THE FUTURE HOLDS IN STORE, I HAVEN'T ANY CLUE. IN MY HUMBLE OPINION, IT DOESN'T SEEM LIKELY THE CREATURES ARE PLANNING ANY KIND OF A COMING-OUT PARTY. THEY RELY TOO HEAVILY ON THEIR SECRECY, BOTH SOCIALLY AND FISCALLY. I CAN'T IMAGINE MERLOTTE'S WOULD PULL IN THE KIND OF BUSINESS IT DOES IF ITS BIBLE-THUMPING, REDNECK CLIENTELE KNEW THE MAN BEHIND BON TEMPS' ONLY BAR CHASES HIS OWN TAIL. SURE, THERE ARE SOME MORE OPEN-MINDED FOLK AROUND HERE, LIKE SOOKIE AND LAFAYETTE, BUT THEN AGAIN, THERE ARE THE OTHERS. THE ARLENES AND THE JASONS AND THE LETTIE MAES. SAM MERLOTTE KNOWS BETTER THAN TO RISK EVERYTHING HE'S BUILT FOR HIMSELF JUST SO HE CAN PUT HIS DOG-AND-PONY SHOW ON DISPLAY FOR THE WHOLE TOWN.

I CAN'T SPEAK TO SHIFTER COMMUNITIES OUTSIDE OF THESE PARTS, AS I HAVE LITTLE TIME OR CONCERN FOR SUCH UNIMPORTANT MATTERS, AND NEVER CARED MUCH FOR PETS (OTHER THAN THE HUMAN KIND). BUT I WILL SAY THAT BON TEMPS IS A HOTBED FOR SUPERNATURAL ACTIVITY, AND THERE IS CERTAINLY NO SHORTAGE OF SHIFTERS (EVEN IF THEY OFTEN END UP . . . DEAD).

****

Merlotte's is closed for the night for the wedding of its own waitress Arlene Fowler and short order cook Terry Bellefleur.

** * * Be sure to wish Terry luck, since it's Arlene's sixth wedding! * * **

****

We will reopen tomorrow with regular business hours

KNOWN ENEMY

NAME Sam Merlotte

SPECIES Shifter

STATUS Active

KNOWN RELATIVES Biological parents Melinda and Joe Lee Mickens, brother Tommy Mickens, adoptive parents Mitch and Sue Ann Merlotte

OCCUPATION Owner and manager of Merlotte's Bar and Grill

GO-TO SHIFT Collie

NOTES

Sam Merlotte was given up for adoption because his mother was only 16 years old and his father was in prison; they didn't feel fit to raise a child. His adoptive parents were thrilled to have their very own son, until Sam hit puberty and involuntarily shifted in front of them. He returned home one day to find that they had moved away, leaving no phone number or address, abandoning him completely. He spent several years moving from place to place, shacking up with all sorts of people, before eventually settling down in Bon Temps and raising enough capital to open up his restaurant. According to a constituent of mine who works the polling place at BT High, Sam voted in favor of the Vampire Rights Amendment. He also has an affinity for Sookie Stackhouse, which makes me wonder if he too is part of this local supernatural domination movement.

Tara used to have a thing with Sam. She said she knew things would never work out for them when she discovered that he barked in his sleep.

THIS TOWN IS SO INCESTUOUS. SAM ALSO USED TO BE IN LOVE WITH SOOKIE. I WONDER IF HE STILL HAS FEELINGS FOR HER OR IF HE'S BURIED THEM DOWN DEEP WITH THE REST OF HIS SECRETS.

Tommy got his ass kicked to death by a bunch of werewolves. I heard it had something to do with skinwalking, which I always thought would be a fun name for a supernatural hooker.

KNOWN ENEMY

NAME Tommy Mickens

SPECIES Shifter

STATUS ~~Active~~

KNOWN RELATIVES Parents Melinda and Joe Lee Mickens, brother Sam Merlotte

OCCUPATION Mechanic/Busboy

GO-TO SHIFT Pit Bull

NOTES

Perhaps Sam's parents weren't wrong when they deemed themselves unfit to raise their first son; they turned out to be truly abhorrent at rearing Tommy, even by shifter standards (although it appears to me that only Melinda is of the shifter nature; Joe Lee is human). Not only did they fail to teach Tommy literacy, they would often make him compete in dogfights in his pit bull form to earn money. This left his body covered with scars and instilled in him a fondness for brute force. When Sam tried to track down his birth parents and first encountered Tommy, both men were shocked to discover they each had a brother. They formed a somewhat tenuous bond, but a bond nonetheless. Under Sam's guidance, Tommy murdered his parents, and I say good riddance to them-the world needs fewer interspecies couples and fewer bad parents! Not long after, Sam actually shot his brother in the leg in an altercation over money, and Tommy moved in with Hoyt Fortenberry's mother Maxine. I can only assume Maxine had no idea the boy was a shifter, as she is a regular churchgoer and charitable woman.

PRIVACY POLICY: SHIFTERS AND WERES

SINCE VAMPIRES CAME OUT OF THE COFFIN, SO TO SPEAK, SHIFTERS AND WERES HAVE MAINTAINED A RATHER QUIET EXISTENCE. FOR REASONS MENTIONED ABOVE, AND FOR REASONS UNMENTIONED, THEY'VE CHOSEN TO KEEP THEIR SUPERNATURAL DISPOSITION HIDDEN FROM THOSE AROUND THEM. INSTEAD OF EMBRACING THEIR LACK OF HUMANITY, AS I DO EVERY SINGLE DAY, THEY DO THEIR DAMNEDEST TO "PASS FOR HUMAN." THIS NEED TO BE PRIVATE IS PROBABLY COMPLEX, COMING FROM A FEAR OF THE IMPLICATIONS OF HUMANS' REACTION TO THEIR KIND, AN AWARENESS AND A PRUDENCE ABOUT THE SUPERNATURAL HIERARCHY, AND SOME SORT OF INSECURITY OR INNER ANTIPATHY. WHEN BILL FIRST ARRIVED IN BON TEMPS, HE EXHIBITED THIS KIND OF SELF-LOATHING AND WAS ALWAYS TRYING TO DENOUNCE HIS VAMPIRIC NATURE AND CHANNEL HIS FORMER MORTAL SELF. BUT LIKE ANY GOOD STUDENT (AND VAMPIRE), BILL FOLLOWED MY LEAD AND LEARNED TO RUN WITH THE BIG BOYS. HOWEVER, SHIFTERS AND WERES LACK THE STRENGTH AND CONFIDENCE—RIGHTLY SO—TO MAKE A BOLD TRANSFORMATION LIKE THIS. IN MY ESTIMATION, BOTH PARTIES WILL REMAIN IN THE CLOSET AS LONG AS THE REST OF THE WORLD LETS THEM.

WITCHES

HISTORY AND LORE

There's a famous line from a pretty "colorful" movie that goes, "Are you a good witch, or a bad witch?" Trust me, it's a trick question. There ain't no such thing as a "good witch."

Liberal revisionists love to reflect on our collective past and claim that famous witch hunts and stake burnings throughout history were instances of misogyny in disguise-an excuse for men to keep women subjugated and enact violence against them in the name of God. While I maintain that women have their proper place in society (let's be honest, things got pretty darn confusing on the gender lines once they started wearing fedoras and smoking cigars), I think our Christian forefathers recognized the difference between a loudmouth who couldn't keep a log cabin clean and a legitimate Bride of Satan.

Witches are like the "nuns" of satanic worship. They have pledged their love to Satan in exchange for access to his unworldly powers. Witches are an ever-increasing threat in our times, as more and more humans are being drawn to the appeal of having supernatural powers and fitting in with the "popular" crowd established by vampires. While the practice of the dark arts does take dedication and focus, becoming a witch is probably one of the easiest and quickest routes to hell. Fathers, lock up your daughters!

That old movie did, however, get one thing right: witches come in many different shapes and sizes. It's one of the reasons the rules of magic are so varying and difficult to nail down. Here are a few examples of the different types of witches:

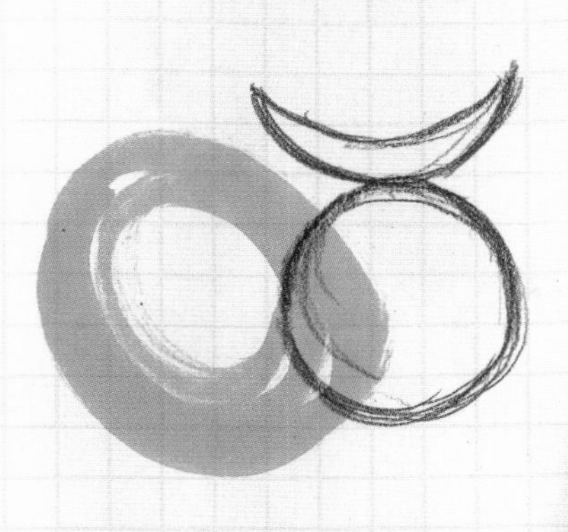

WICCANS

Let us not mince words. "Wicca" is simply another name for "witchcraft," which came into popularity during the second half of the 20th century as yet another example of rebranding an old evil to give it a friendlier face and therefore more mass appeal. You can put lipstick on an old hag on a broomstick, but a Wiccan is still just a witch.

Wiccans are tree-hugging pagans who primarily worship two deities, a female "moon goddess," and a male "horned God" (hmmm . . . who else has horns?). Wiccans have learned to manipulate what they regard as a naturally occurring force of nature, known as "magick," to impose their will over the laws of physics and unlock deeper mysteries of the universe. Where this magic comes from or what it means is still not understood, and is generally disregarded by the layman, but it is possible that it is simply some law in accordance of the universe that scientists and theologians have yet to fully discover and define. Myself, I'm pretty sure it's the power of Satan. Though many Wiccans present themselves as helpers and healers of mankind who are in tune with nature, the truth is they've been metaphysically sleeping with the wrong guy and now they've picked up a nasty supernatural STD.

Wiccans typically gather together in a sisterhood, or a coven, to perform pagan rituals, cast spells, curse their enemies, and in some cases, raise the dead. One of America's most famous covens of witches took over Salem, Massachusetts from 1692 to 1693, until the God-abiding men of law and order exposed them for the Satan-loving succubae they were and had them tried and executed to the resounding cheers of the Christian people. And yet, we still celebrate Halloween every year. What is wrong with this country?

WARLOCKS AND WIZARDS

Male counterparts of witches. These conjurers are the priests of the damned. Since they have aligned themselves with such a womanly supernatural pursuit, they are probably into things like cross-dressing, mimosa brunches, and designer sweatpants.

Add a human in a dog collar and it sounds like my kind of party.

NECROMANCERS

Necromancers are witches of the darkest order. They have delved so deeply into the dark arts that they have learned to contact and even manipulate the dead. Since vampires are technically animated corpses, it is possible for necromancers to take control of vampires and use them to do their bidding. Now, in the right hands, necromancy could be a very powerful weapon in the war against vampires, but I don't feel like going down on the devil just so I can make a skeleton dance the Charleston.

BRUJOS

Brujos are Latin American witches, both male and female, who have recently been flooding this country in startling numbers, practicing their witchcraft in hotels, almond farms, fast food restaurants, and the homes of wealthy families. If left unattended, these practitioners of brujería will soon replace all American witches, and everyone in this country will recognize Spanish as our national language.

ALCHEMISTS

Alchemy is a form of magical practice that derives from the ancient hermetic tradition of controlling the material world through supernatural forces. Alchemists are warlocks in lab coats, tinkering away at the fabric of God's work, through the transmogrification and manipulation of matter with magic. The early alchemists were mostly interested in turning metal into gold (I guess in order to beef up Satan's bank account) while later generations went as far as creating artificial life itself from the materials of the earth, such as mud or clay. With its roots in the basic elements of chemistry, biology, and philosophy, alchemy stands as proof that all explorations in the field of science are ultimately untrustworthy.

VOODOO QUEENS

Voodoo is a type of folk magic that was brought over to Louisiana from Africa. Voodoo queens practice conjuring supernatural deities and employing otherworldly forces to spice up their love lives, fix their financial woes, and curse their enemies. Voodoo queens are also known to have the ability to see into the future, exorcise demons from the bodies of the possessed, and decorate skulls with top hats. Pretty standard non-Christian activity-Satan-worshipping disguised as exotic import.

Jesus and Lafayette: A Brujomance

Steve clearly didn't do his research . . . Brujeria is some serious shit. It's witchcraft from south of the border, and like the food (or so I've heard), it's spicier than a Naga Viper pepper. It has nothing to do with tourism, nut farms, or junk food joints like Newlin suggested. I got a firsthand account of this form of magic from Lafayette's little boy toy, a bum bandit born and bred a brujo in Catemaco, Veracruz in Mexico.

One day a few years ago, I ventured into Merlotte's on business from Eric (he wanted to redo the Fangtasia website and thought Lafayette might have some web advice since he had once had such a successful online career), where I ran into Jesus Velasquez, nursing a beer and waiting for his boyfriend to get off work. He struck up a conversation with me, and while I usually ignore humans interested in engaging my attention, something about his energy intrigued me. So naturally, I glamoured him and in no time, he spilled his guts on the table. He told me about the time his mother caught his grandfather, Don Bartolo (sounds like the name of a cheap tequila), teaching him black magic, how he and his mother spent the rest of his adolescence traipsing around the globe together, how they eventually settled down in Louisiana. He explained that he had tried to avoid magic–even denounce it –for years, fearing his grandfather's power and influence. But upon nursing Ruby Jean Reynolds and meeting her son, Lafayette, his spirit was awakened and he wanted to revisit his roots. See, he was convinced that Lafayette possessed an inherent aptitude for brujeria. Of course I thought it all sounded ridiculous at the time, but then all the Marnie shit hit the fan, and it turned out magic was alive and well in Shreveport. Since then, Lafayette's managed to start another business, as a sorcerous medium for hire for the likes of errant waitresses and bored housewives. I'm not sure if he has a website yet, but if he does, I'm sure it's award-worthy. That cock jockey's got a flair for magic and web design.

The most powerful of the brujos, according to Jesus, is the medium. This is a special role reserved for only the most exceptional magic practitioners, and involves direct communication with the dead. Some mediums simply exchange messages with the deceased, while others, like Lafayette, can actually be possessed by spirits of bitches who just don't know when to quit. Jesus, in his longwindedness, also shared a little bit about the history of brujeria with me. He said the term brujo had taken on so many negative connotations due to its historical notoriety, that some of his brethren started calling themselves curanderos, which is Spanish for healer (ironic, though, because it can also be translated as quack, a term for halfwits posing as trained doctors). While most brujos practice their arts and use their powers–via spells, incantations, concoctions, bloodletting–to harm those around them or for personal gains, much like Jesus' grandfather, Jesus was convinced not all brujos have ill intentions. I'm inclined to think anyone practicing magic has a hard-on for trouble, but then again, Lafayette and I have learned to get along despite our differences, and I'm increasingly impressed by his wardrobe choices. So who am I to judge if he likes Ouija boards and the occasional séance? That said, the actual practice of this kind of witchcraft is hard to pin down, as there are differing forms and rituals that are often passed down through generations and guarded like family heirlooms. But with Lafayette back in the cruising lane now that Jesus is gone, I have to wonder if the Velasquez magic died with him . . .

The Velasquez family magic, when conjured up to its most powerful version, manifests in the form of a demon-like mask. If you ask me, it looks like something you'd see on Santa Monica Boulevard during West Hollywood's Halloween parade . . .

WHAT GOES DOWN AT MOONGODDESS EMPORIUM

December 5

While taking notes on the local supernatural activity in Shreveport today, I stumbled upon a quaint New Age bookstore called MoonGoddess Emporium. It is the type of curio shop that sells crystal pyramids and CDs of pan flute music, and stinks of patchouli and rosemary oil. We had a similar place in Dallas called the Lotus Drop, that was next door to Sarah's and my favorite Mexican restaurant, and in which Sarah enjoyed poking around after a pitcher of margaritas. Never my scene, but Sarah is into all that smelly stuff, and one time I did happen to find a nice windsock featuring Michelangelo's Creation of Adam. It's still flapping around next to the garage (unless Sarah torched it with the rest of my stuff, which is very probably the case).

Anyhoo, it's been rather hot and humid for this time of year, and I had been walking down the block looking to quench my growing thirst with a Vanilla Coke Slurpee, when I noticed MoonGoddess Emporium and decided to poke my head in. The owner is a jittery, middle-aged woman who rarely looked me in the eye (I kind of got the sense she isn't really into men-she wore a sleeveless top, exposing her armpits, and let's just say her hedges could have used some trimming). She has a wide collection of pagan reading materials, and when I asked her if she was a witch, she said, "We don't really call ourselves that anymore." Uh huh. Well, she seemed harmless enough, so I quickly perused an assortment of Celtic themed pinwheels and then excused myself and made my way down the block to the 7-Eleven.

With nothing else going on tonight, I decided to stake the place out. Around 10:00 P.M., I witnessed a small collection of people, mostly 20 year-olds, with a few in their 30s and 40s, maybe, enter the shop and disappear into a back room. Merlotte's waitress Holly Cleary was among them, confirming my suspicions about her Wiccan tendencies. Honestly, they just looked like a bunch of nice kids who needed a good prayer group. Misguided, perhaps, but innocent-seeming nonetheless. Around 11:00 P.M., they came out, exchanged pleasantries, and went home. No sign of trouble. In fact, the entire episode was pretty innocuous. Now, I don't know what went on back there, but I have my doubts that nervous nelly of a shop owner could command a coven that could pose any real kind of threat. Then again, maybe that's what the devil wants me to believe.

Believe it, bitch. Marnie Stonebrook may look like a plain-faced, granola-cruncher at a Sarah McLachlan concert, but she turned out to be the real deal.

KNOWN ENEMY

NAME: Marnie Stonebrook

SPECIES: Witch

STATUS: Six feet under

KNOWN RELATIVES: A conure named Minerva

OCCUPATION: Owner of MoonGoddess Emporium Wicca shop

NOTES:

Not only did this c-word place a curse on me that left my flesh rotting from the inside out, she managed to magically neuter Eric, transforming him from a Viking sex warrior into a high school virgin who worked the night shift at Puppies "R" Us. Marnie had harnessed the power of some ancient witch named Antonia, who apparently was pissed because some asshole vampire priests burned her at the stake a few centuries back (get over it, lady-men suck, and not just the vampires). So her spirit used Marnie as a vessel to cast a spell to draw vampires out of the ground during the day to "meet the sun." Naturally, Eric, Bill, that redheaded tween-flavored piece of jailbait he calls a progeny, and I rolled up to MoonGoddess with black leather and a bazooka and almost blew the joint sky-high. We would have, too, if it weren't for some spell that protected the building. Honestly, this magic stuff is all just show. If these Wiccan bitches want to take on vampires, they need to drop some Lilith Fair-sized balls and quit hiding behind their fireworks. I'll happily take them on. I could use a new set of toothpicks.

NECROMANCY AND VAMPIRES

PAM THINKS THAT BRUJERÍA IS A FORCE TO BE RECKONED WITH? DEMON MASKS AND ANIMAL SACRIFICES ARE CHILD'S PLAY, AND ONLY CONCERN THE PETTY DESIRES OF HUMANS. NECROMANCY IS THE REAL THREAT AGAINST VAMPIRES.
NECROMANCY IS A FORM OF MAGIC THAT PRE-DATES THE 17TH CENTURY AND ITS HEYDAY DURING THE SPANISH INQUISITION. IT REACHES ALL THE WAY BACK TO WESTERN ANTIQUITY, TO THE DAYS OF ANCIENT EGYPT AND BABYLON. THIS DARK MAGIC GRANTS THE BEHOLDER THE POWER TO RAISE THE DEAD, TO CONTROL THE DEAD, AND SINCE VAMPIRES ARE, WELL, DEAD . . . YOU GET THE POINT.

I PERSONALLY DISCOVERED WHAT IT'S LIKE TO BE AT GROUND ZERO OF A NECROMANCER'S OPUS. I WALKED INTO MARNIE'S TRAP ARROGANT (AS I'M WONT TO BE FROM TIME TO TIME), UNDER THE ASSUMPTION A LOCAL COVEN OF WITCHES COULD HOLD NO SWAY OVER VAMPIRES. KING COMPTON, WHO HAD SENT ME TO SUSS OUT MOONGODDESS EMPORIUM, HAD WARNED ME THEY WERE NECROMANCERS, BUT SINCE THE AVL HADN'T OFFICIALLY SIGNED OFF ON THE INVESTIGATION, I ASSUMED THEIR CLAIMS TO MAGIC WERE FALSE AND THAT THEY WERE SOMEHOW BLUFFING. WHAT I DIDN'T KNOW WAS THAT MARNIE STONEBROOK WAS JUST MASTERING THE ART OF NECROMANCY, AND WOULD SOON BE POSSESSED BY A SPIRIT MORE HEINOUS THAN PAM'S ROTTING FACE.

THE LAST THING I REMEMBER, BEFORE MY MEMORY WENT OUT LIKE A LIGHTBULB, WAS A CHANT. ELEMENTS OF THE NIGHT, ELEMENTS OF THE DEAD, COME THIS WAY, WE CALL UPON YE, WE SUMMON YE. THEN MARNIE WHIPPED OUT SOME LATIN, WHICH I HAVE TO ADMIT BROUGHT ON A VAGUE SENSE OF NOSTALGIA FOR MY DAYS AS A BABY VAMP: JAM TIBI IMPERO ET PRAECIPIO MALIGNE SPIRITUS! ROUGHLY TRANSLATED, IT MEANS, "NOW I COMMAND AND CHARGE YOU, OH EVIL SPIRIT!" WHAT SHE SAID AFTER THAT? I HAVE NO IDEA. IT WAS IN THAT MOMENT I WAS ERASED AND REPLACED WITH A WEAK AND SUBMISSIVE MAN, TRANSFORMED INTO A HAND PUPPET FOR ANTONIA GAVILÁN DE LOGROÑO, A 17TH CENTURY WITCH WITH A LONG-STANDING GRUDGE AGAINST VAMPIRE KIND.

IT WAS SOOKIE WHO SAVED ME. SHE FOUND ME, HELPED ME, FOUGHT FOR ME, AND EVENTUALLY LOVED ME. I WISH I COULD REMEMBER WHAT THAT WAS LIKE, BUT ALAS, THOSE MEMORIES DIED WHEN I WAS FREED OF MARNIE'S SPELL. PERHAPS THE MOST DISTURBING PART OF THIS EPISODE ISN'T THAT CONTROL OVER MYSELF WAS SO EASILY RELINQUISHED, BUT WHO I'M TOLD I BECAME UNDER THE SPELL. WAS THAT LOYAL LAPDOG SO DESPERATE TO BE LOVED A BYPRODUCT OF MY CURSE, OR A PIECE OF THE ERIC NORTHMAN I'VE BURIED DEEP INSIDE THE ARMOR OF A 1,000 YEAR-OLD VIKING WARRIOR? I TRY NOT TO REFLECT ON IT TOO MUCH. INTROSPECTION IS FOR PUSSIES AND NAVEL-GAZERS.

HAVING LIVED THROUGH THE INQUISITION, HAVING SEEN WITCHES CAST A SPELL POWERFUL ENOUGH TO DRAW VAMPIRES INTO THE SUN, HAVING BEEN THE VERY VICTIM OF THIS BLACK MAGIC, I TAKE THE THREAT OF NECROMANCERS VERY SERIOUSLY. AND NOW THAT YOU'RE A VAMPIRE, STEVE, SO SHOULD YOU.

That's my "mourning" look. I was grieving for my beautiful face. Despite the beekeeper resemblance, I must say, I look damn good in black.

AND YET, THERE'S MORE

Vampires, weres, and shifters . . . oh my! What else is out there?

My heart breaks in half whenever I think of all those poor souls from pre-mainstreaming times, who were attacked by vampires and had no one to turn to, for fear of looking like a wacko.

This is why the work we do at the Fellowship of the Sun is so important. As the church's mission expands into PHASE 2, we will expand counseling and education to provide a safe haven not just for victims of vampire attacks, but for folks who have encountered unclassified cryptids. Already in the past few months, more and more terrified Christians have come our way with eyewitness accounts and firsthand experiences of other creatures, currently classified as "imaginary."

You may want to buckle your seat belts, folks, what I am about to describe will enlighten and terrify.

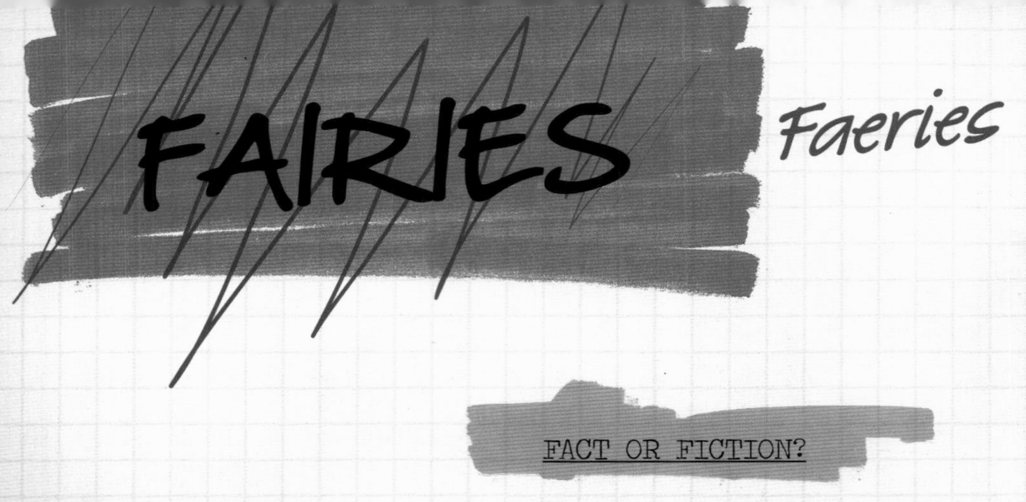

Faeries

FACT OR FICTION?

As we fall further down the rabbit hole, where do the worlds of reality and fiction meet? Just how many different kinds of monsters are out there . . . and are they all evil?

Take the ~~fairy~~ faerie, for example.

In James Willingbum's engaging book Unimaginable: A Case for the Fairy, the author* points to historical accounts of human/~~fairy~~ faerie interaction, mainly during the Middle Ages. The Brotherhood of the Eternal Sun, for example, told of an encounter with a ~~fairy~~ faerie queen who "shot forth rays of light betwixt her fingers," and "stole away with one of their members to a strange realm. There he was offered glowing, radiant fruit that frightened him and the ~~fairy~~ faerie queen only returned him to our world after he swore an oath to slay a demon that was hunting her." Willingbum points to the Cottingley ~~Fairy~~ Faerie case, where, in 1917, two young girls were photographed with ~~fairies~~ faeries they had encountered in their aunt's garden, as an incident "in need of reexamination since vampires have opened the doorway to the supernatural world."

* Despite Willingbum being a homosexual English professor from Oxford (I've always been skeptical about gay Americans, so I'm pretty sure one shouldn't look a gay UN-American in the eye), his delicate words and strong jawline (as depicted on the inside dust cover photograph) suggested that he was a man of intellect and intelligence, so I picked up his book. Later that year, I was fortunate to meet James at a book signing at a Dallas Barnes & Noble. He was familiar with my work and we struck up a neighborly debate on what John kept calling the "reclassification of the human race in a supernatural world." He was certainly critical of my stance against vampires (did I mention he was a flaming liberal as well?), but as he yammered on about how humanity is entering a "hyper-Romantic age," I found myself unable to avert my attention from his charming character, impeccable dress, and mellifluous English accent. He was perhaps the most skilled orator I'd met since my father. Our conversation carried us to dinner at the Olive Garden next door, where he told me stories of his upbringing in Gloucester and explained the rules of cricket. We must have been hitting it off, because I somehow ended up in his hotel room, where the conversation eventually extinguished as the evening was taken over by a CSI Miami marathon and an increasingly awkward silence. After an hour or two, he said he had to catch a plane in the morning, so I humbly excused myself. I drove home, crawled into bed with Sarah, and realized I had left my signed copy of James's book on his hotel room desk.

So what makes a ~~fairy~~ faerie? I imagine they would be hard to detect since they are so small, perhaps only seen at night when the light from their glowing flesh can be spotted. They may or may not exude some kind of dust or dandruff that gives the power of flight when sprinkled over human flesh.

~~Fairies~~ Faeries are often depicted as wish granters or guardian angels, so it's possible these beings are working for the Good Lord. However, more often than not, these tiny sprites are said to abduct human babies from their beds, torture livestock, and lead men into ~~fairy~~ faerie circles where they are transported to other worlds, never to be seen again, which makes them very similar to sinister aliens from other planets.

All of this seems a bit silly, and despite James Willingbum's grace upon the page, I can safely presume that ~~fairies~~ faeries remain the work of childish imaginations and Walt Disney.

THOSE FAERIE FUCKERS

Vampires aren't supposed to have feelings. We're meant to remorselessly suck the blood of humans and sometimes bed them and then be on our merry way. Whether or not you believe in Lilith or God or Charles Manson or in Jesse fucking Jackson, that was the sole reason we were put on this earth.

But I've witnessed what I suppose I might call Armageddon or the apocalypse, to borrow a few terms from Steve: Eric Northman being henpecked into a purse-carrying, heart-shaped-pancake-making, feelings kind of guy. Is it because of love? Fuck no. It's because of that bottle blonde Sookie Stackhouse's faerie blood. One whiff of her insides and Eric hasn't been the same since.

Faeries were once just characters of—yep—fairy tales. Mythological creatures that, if they ever existed, had gone extinct centuries ago. Vampires often called them the Old People, but they were also known as finodrerr, ellyllon, las anjanas, daoine sidhe, even aliens. But since the halfling Stackhouse appeared at our doorstep in that little sundress, rupturing my once-perfect union with Eric, the legend has come back to life. Or back to earth, I should say. It turns out faeries never went extinct, but instead escaped through a portal to a different plane when their population started to dwindle. They called this place the Land of the Fae, and there they remained, biding their time, dancing in skimpy getups, procreating with unknowing humans, and hiding from vampires.

I can't say I blame them for avoiding us—their blood offers vampires the one thing we can't have: daywalking. It's a slippery slope, though. Faerie blood only gives us the ability to walk in the sun for a few minutes at a time. After that, we crisp up like charred hamburgers at a backyard BBQ. While most vampires dream of daywalking, salivating for some time in the sun, it's not something worth damaging my near-perfect skin over, nor is it something that ever appealed to me much, even in my human days. I suppose I was always a creature of the night, working in a bordello and all . . . But this isn't about me. This is about Sookie and her stupid, annoying, exceedingly

Hi! my name's Sookie and I make sparkles!!

The stench of cheap perfume.

Should be dead by now.

tiresome faerie blood. I had secretly (or not so secretly) hoped that during her "missing year," she would be gone from our lives forever. But when she resurfaced, revealing that not only was she alive and well, but her kind were alive and well in abundance, let's just say I had to let off some steam. And by let off some steam, I mean grab a few of Ginger's girlfriends, take them down to the saw room, and have my way with them.

A REBUTTAL ON THE SUBJECT OF THE FAE

PAM, JEALOUS PAM. SHE DOESN'T LIKE WHEN I FIND OTHER WOMEN TO PLAY WITH. IT'S A SHAME SHE'S LETTING HER EMOTIONS (IF ONE BELIEVES PAMELA IS EVEN CAPABLE OF HAVING EMOTIONS) BLIND HER FROM THE TRUE BEAUTY AND SIGNIFICANCE OF FAERIES. IN THOSE BRIEF MOMENTS WITH SUNLIGHT ON MY FACE, I FELT A WARMTH, A VITALITY, THAT HAD BEEN MISSING SINCE THE TIME I SPENT AT THE NORTH SEA AS A BOY. IT IS NOT AN ERA I MISS—I DO NOT PINE FOR MY HUMAN YEARS—BUT I PINE FOR THAT WARMTH. I HADN'T SEEN DAYLIGHT FOR OVER A MILLENNIUM, AND MY BODY HAS SUFFERED. MY SKIN HAS GROWN COLD, SOOKIE EVEN SAYS MY SOUL HAS GROWN COLD. PERHAPS SHE'S RIGHT.

IT IS STILL COMMONLY ACCEPTED WITHIN THE VAMPIRE COMMUNITY THAT FAERIES ARE THE STUFF OF LEGEND. SO WHEN I FIRST TOOK IN THE SMELL OF SOOKIE'S BLOOD THE NIGHT BILL BROUGHT HER TO FANGTASIA, IT WAS NOTHING SHORT OF A SHOCK TO MY SYSTEM. AFTER CENTURIES OF BELIEVING THE FAE HAD GONE EXTINCT, THAT DAYWALKING WAS MERELY A MYTH OF OUR FOREFATHERS, HERE WAS A HALFLING, WALKING INTO MY BAR IN A TART LITTLE ENSEMBLE. IT WAS LOVE AT FIRST SCENT; THE FUTURE WAS FULL OF . . . POSSIBILITY. I'M NOT SURE HOW I MADE IT THIS LONG WITHOUT HAVING ENCOUNTERED A FAERIE, BUT THEN AGAIN, VERY FEW OF THEM WOULD COME NEAR THE LIKES OF ME. FORTUNATELY MOST OF THE VAMPIRES IN MY BAR THAT NIGHT WERE TOO YOUNG TO EVEN IDENTIFY THAT INTOXICATING FRAGRANCE OR UNDERSTAND ITS MAGNITUDE.

IF BROADCAST FAR AND WIDE, THE DISCOVERY THAT FAERIES INDEED EXIST—AND THAT SOME OF THEM ARE EVEN AMONG US ON THIS PLANE—WOULD LITERALLY BLOW THE MINDS OF VAMPIRES, ESPECIALLY THOSE AS OLD AS I AM.

THERE IS SO MUCH TO EXPLORE ABOUT FAERIES . . .

TELEPATHY: FAERIES CAN READ THE MINDS OF HUMANS, SHIFTERS, AND WERES, BUT FORTUNATELY (OR PERHAPS UNFORTUNATELY), NOT OF VAMPIRES.

LIGHT: FAERIES CAN SHOOT LIGHT FROM THEIR FINGERS THAT IS POTENT ENOUGH TO SUBDUE MAENADS, VAMPIRES, AND EVEN THE MOST POWERFUL OF WITCHES' SPELLS.

TIME: SOOKIE CLAIMS SHE WAS IN THE LAND OF THE FAE FOR ONLY 10 MINUTES, BUT TIME MUST BE DIFFERENT ON THAT PLANE; SHE HAD BEEN MISSING FROM OUR WORLD FOR 12½ MONTHS.

LIGHT FRUIT: FAERIES TRIED TO FEED SOOKIE A "LUMIERE," BUT BECAUSE SHE CHOSE NOT TO EAT IT, SHE WAS ABLE TO ESCAPE THROUGH THE PORTAL AND RETURN HOME.

LET'S KEEP THESE DETAILS IN THE FAMILY, SHALL WE? I DON'T WANT TO HAVE TO PROTECT SOOKIE FROM EVERY VAMPIRE TOM, DICK, AND HARRY CHASING DOWN HER BLOOD LIKE HORNY TEENAGERS. MOST VAMPIRES DON'T HAVE THE SELF-CONTROL THAT BILL AND I EXHIBIT. WE ARE STRONGER; WE HAVE A WILL POWER THAT GOES BEYOND IMMEDIATE GRATIFICATION, SOMETHING RARE FOR OUR KIND. I REALIZE I LET THIS GUARD DOWN WHEN I ACCIDENTALLY DRAINED SOOKIE'S FAERIE GODMOTHER CLAUDINE, BUT THEN AGAIN, I WASN'T REALLY MYSELF . . .

ALL OF THIS FAE BUSINESS RAISES A VERY INTERESTING AND POTENTIALLY LUCRATIVE QUESTION: CAN WE SYNTHESIZE FAERIE BLOOD? IF SO, VAMPIRES COULD WALK THE EARTH DAY AND NIGHT. OUR ACHILLES' HEEL WOULD NO LONGER EXIST; THE HUMAN ADVANTAGE WOULD BE NO MORE. BRILLIANT SCIENTISTS FOUND A WAY TO SYNTHESIZE HUMAN BLOOD, AND TRU BLOOD IS NOW A HOUSEHOLD NAME. WHO'S TO SAY THEY CAN'T DO THE SAME WITH FAERIE BLOOD? IF YOU THROW ENOUGH MONEY AT ANY PROBLEM, SOMEONE'S BOUND TO SOLVE IT.

OTHER CREATURES OF SATAN IN SOUTHERN FOLKLORE

SKUNK APE

The skunk ape is a Bigfoot-like creature that is said to lurk in the swamps and wetlands of Louisiana, Georgia, and the Florida panhandle. This big bubba is related to the more famous North American Bigfoot, and gets his name from the horrible stench that precedes his arrival. One of our newest members who came to us from Niceville, Florida, Cindy Bateman, spotted this 8-foot beauty contest reject going through her garbage cans as she arrived home from the bingo hall one night. Cindy, at first believing the gruesome giant was a bear, grabbed her shotgun from the passenger seat and fired at it. The blast grazed the man-killer's shoulder, and when it spun around to look at the source of the shot, Cindy could see his human-like face and glowing red eyes. The beast quickly disappeared into the night with a half-gallon of expired milk and an old potato. Cindy claims the creature's stench hung in the air until the next morning, when she awoke to find all seven of her cats had gone blind.

MOTHMAN

This demonic creature is said to have reigned over Point Pleasant, West Virginia for the past four decades. Named after its large head with glowing, saucer-like eyes and large wings, this flying monster propels itself down lonely highways at night and typically portends some personal or communal disaster. In other words, seeing this guy is bad luck. Harold and Carol Conwurst, two recent recruits to the FOTS, claimed this monster followed their pickup for five miles down the highway last November, and at one point latched onto the roof of their vehicle, scraping at the cab with talon-like hands, before finally giving up and disappearing into the night. Horrified and shaken, the Conwursts headed home only to discover the beast waiting for them in a tree alongside their driveway, where Harold claims it "barked at us with a high-pitched, coughing-like wail. It sounded like the poor bastard was suffering from some horrible form of bronchitis. I almost took pity on it." The Conwursts pulled out of the driveway and spent the night in a motel. Three weeks later, their home was flooded when a water main broke, destroying all of their possessions, including Harold's complete run of something called Peepers magazine and Carol's full set of Precious Moments collectibles. Nine months after the sighting, the Conwursts gave birth to a baby with a tail.

LIZARD MEN

From another class of strange creatures come the lizard men. These blood-sucking, crocodiley beasts walk upright, like humans, and are said to take shelter in swamps and underground tunnels. Some people go so far as to claim that these mysterious creatures can shape-shift to look like humans, and may in fact be demons from another dimension sent to take over the planet in secret. Is this the next level in satanic strategy? Some sort of reptilian, vampire-shifter hybrid? Bob Reed, a deacon at the church, thinks so. He claims to have seen one of these monsters standing over his bed one night. Frozen with fear, Bob watched as the reptoid shape shifted into George Washington and then made sexual advances towards him. Bob blacked out, but in the morning found two-fang marks on his neck. Now it's possible that this memory could have been the result of a cruel glamouring prank played on Bob by some distasteful vampires, but Bob claims he's never invited a vampire into his house! Public record shows he was once arrested for taking V, but he asserts he was framed and thought he was just buying some medicinal marijuana for his cancer-ridden mother. And you know what? I believe him. Bob's a good guy, an honest man of God, so if he says he saw a lizard man, then he saw a lizard man. Ah, wouldn't you just love the chance to turn one of these bastards into a fine pair of crocodile boots? I know I would!

CHUPACABRA

This threat is another reason we need to work harder at securing our borders. An immigrant from Mexico, this 2-foot-tall creature has been spotted throughout Texas and the southwest. Also known as "the goatsucker," El Chupacabra is responsible for increasing exsanguinations of the livestock of unsuspecting ranchers across the land. A ranch hand from El Paso once told me he spotted this spiked, black-eyed creature draining blood from the neck of a dead calf. He tried sneaking up and capturing the creature with a snare, but it moved so quickly that it shot out into the night before he could say boo! Could the Chupacabra be some Latin American distant cousin of the vampire? Perhaps these beasts are the vampires of the animal kingdom? I say it's likely. Satan has probably sent forth these minions to destroy our food supply in order to make us weaker and less resilient to vampire attacks. Well, not on my watch, Lucifer!

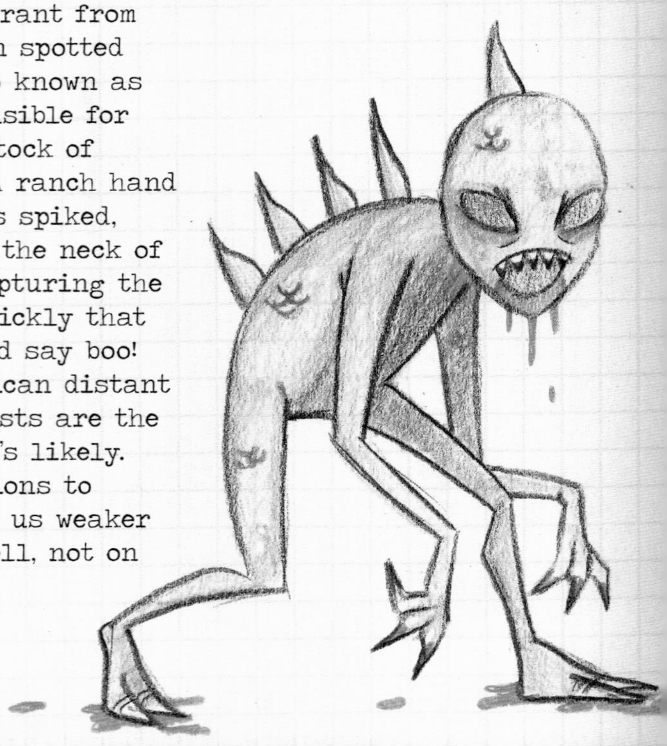

OTHER "CREATURES OF SATAN" IN BON TEMPS AND THE SURROUNDING AREAS

SOUTHERN FOLKLORE CAN KISS MY PALE, NORDIC ASS. MOTHMEN AND CHUPACABRAS MAY HAUNT THE MINDS OF LITTLE CHILDREN TELLING SPOOKY CAMPFIRE STORIES, BUT BON TEMPS HAS BEEN PLAGUED BY A VAST ARRAY OF SUPERNATURAL CREATURES THAT ACTUALLY EXIST. I'M NOT SURE I WOULD CALL THEM ALL CREATURES OF SATAN, BUT THERE ARE SOME I PROBABLY HATE AS MUCH AS STEVE DID WHEN HE FIRST SET OUT TO WRITE THIS BOOK . . .

GHOSTS

SPECTERS, GHOULS, APPARITIONS. GHOSTS ARE SPIRITS OF THE DECEASED IN SEARCH OF SOME SORT OF PEACE. I FEEL A LITTLE SORRY FOR THEM. UNLIKE VAMPIRES, THEY GET ALL THE DEATH AND NONE OF THE FUN. SOME OF THEM APPEAR TO THE LIVING IN THE FORM OF A TRANSLUCENT PHANTOM, WHILE OTHERS CHOOSE NOT TO BE SEEN, BUT ONLY HEARD. OUR RECENT VISITORS HAVE INCLUDED A FEW OF THE BENEVOLENT SORT: MAVIS IN SEARCH OF HER MURDERED CHILD, ADELE STACKHOUSE TRYING TO WARN HER GRANDDAUGHTER SOOKIE, JESUS VELASQUEZ VISITING LAFAYETTE FOR A GOODNIGHT KISS. AND OTHERS, OF COURSE, ARE FAR FROM BENIGN: ANTONIA GAVILÁN DE LOGROÑO, MARNIE STONEBROOK, RENE LENIER.

GHOSTS ARE UNABLE TO MANIPULATE THE TANGIBLE WORLD, BUT THEY HAVE THE ABILITY TO POSSESS HUMANS AND INFLUENCE THEM TO DO THEIR BIDDING. THE HUMANS THEY POSSESS, HOWEVER, MUST BE MEDIUMS, SUSCEPTIBLE TO COMMUNING WITH THE DEAD. SOMETIMES THIS BOND IS A MUTUAL AND CONSENSUAL ONE, WHILE AT OTHER TIMES, IT IS BY FORCE. THE MORE POWERFUL THE MEDIUM, THE MORE THEY CAN NEGOTIATE WITH LOOMING SPIRITS.

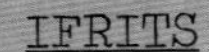

IFRITS

No confirmed infomation about them

THE LATEST CRAZE IN THE BON TEMPS SUPERNATURAL SCENE, THE IFRIT IS A FIRE DEMON FROM THE MIDDLE EASTERN TRADITION, TYPICALLY BORNE OF BLOOD AND GRIEF AND SUMMONED THROUGH A CURSE. ALL-CONSUMING, EXTREMELY POWERFUL, AND COMPOSED ALMOST ENTIRELY OF SMOKE, THE IFRIT DOES NOT ATTACK WILDLY OR AT RANDOM. IT HAS A VERY SPECIFIC TARGET: THE CURSED PARTY (USUALLY A VIOLENT AGGRESSOR—A MURDERER OR RAPIST). IT CANNOT BE EXTINGUISHED UNTIL IT HAS EXTRACTED REVENGE UPON THE WORTHLESS MEAT-SACK THAT INVOKED ITS WRATH. HUMANS DO NOT STAND A CHANCE AGAINST IFRITS, BUT SOME SAY THAT MAGIC CAN WRESTLE WITH THESE DEMONS.

IMP SHALOOPS

No confirmed infomation about them

AND YOU THOUGHT "IFRIT" WAS A RIDICULOUS NAME? IMP SHALOOPS ARE TRICKSTER SPIRITS THAT FEED OFF HUMANS IN VARIOUS WAYS. THEY ARE BLOOD DRINKERS WITH FANGS AND JAWS THAT UNHINGE AND OPEN MUCH FARTHER THAN THOSE OF VAMPIRES. THEY CAN GROW LARGE TENTACLES FROM THEIR BACKS THAT WRAP AROUND HUMANS, ALLOWING THEM TO DRAIN THEIR LIFE FORCE. THEY LOVE A GOOD STORY, AND FATTEN THEMSELVES UP ON SHAME, HUMILIATION, AND BURIED SECRETS OF THEIR VICTIMS. I'VE ENCOUNTERED A FEW OF THESE GUYS OVER THE YEARS, MOST RECENTLY ONE NAMED TED, WHO MADE A SHITTY NIGHT EVEN SHITTIER. IT WAS ALSO RUMORED THAT LIAM, A LOCAL VAMPIRE THAT HAD AN AFFAIR WITH MAUDETTE PICKENS, RENE LENIER'S FIRST VICTIM IN BON TEMPS, MAY HAVE ACTUALLY BEEN AN IMP SHALOOP (THE TENTACLE TATTOO ON HIS BACK WAS A BIT OF A GIVEAWAY, NOT TO MENTION HE MOVED IN VERY STRANGE WAYS), BUT HE WAS DESTROYED IN A FIRE BEFORE ANY SUSPICIONS COULD BE PROPERLY CONFIRMED.

MAENADS

AHH, MY LEAST FAVORITE OF THE BUNCH. THE IMMORTAL, ANCIENT HANDMAIDENS OF DIONYSUS, AND SERIOUS PARTY CRASHERS THAT DON'T SEEM TO UNDERSTAND WHAT IT MEANS TO BE PERSONA NON GRATA. THEY ARE NEARLY IMPOSSIBLE TO KILL; BULLETS CANNOT EVEN PENETRATE THESE CREATURES, THEY WILL INSTEAD DEFLECT THEM, RICOCHETING OFF INTO INNOCENT BYSTANDERS.

KNOWN BY OTHER NAMES LIKE ISIS AND KALI, MAENADS HAVE THE POWER TO CONTROL HUMANS, PUTTING THEM UNDER A SPELL THAT TURNS THEM INTO HEDONISTIC FOOLS WHO CAN'T REMEMBER A DAMN THING. I SUPPOSE IT'S NOT ENTIRELY UNLIKE WHEN I WAS UNDER THE NECROMANCER'S SPELL . . . ONLY I DIDN'T ENGAGE IN AN ORGY WITH THE ENTIRE TOWN OF BON TEMPS, JANE BODEHOUSE INCLUDED. MAENADS ARE UTTERLY DEVOTED TO SUMMONING A DEITY THEY CALL THE GOD WHO COMES AND TO PAYING HOMAGE TO THEIR IDOLIZED DIONYSUS, AND THEY BELIEVE SACRIFICING A SUPERNATURAL BEING IS THE WAY TO ACCOMPLISH THIS. UNFORTUNATELY FOR SAM MERLOTTE, MARYANN SEEMED TO HOLD A CANDLE FOR HIM.

THEY MAY SOUND LIKE RIDICULOUS CREATURES, WHAT WITH THE FRENZIED EYES AND DEBAUCHED PARTIES, BUT MAENADS ARE DANGEROUS. THEY HAVE CLAWS THAT CAN POISON A HUMAN INTO PARALYSIS, AND EVEN VAMPIRE BLOOD CANNOT HEAL THE INJURY. IN FACT, MAENAD BLOOD IS SO TOXIC TO VAMPIRES THAT WHEN BILL TOOK A CHOMP OUT OF OUR LITTLE FRIEND MARYANN, HE NEARLY CHOKED TO THE TRUE DEATH.

KNOWN ENEMY

NAME: MARYANN FORRESTER
SPECIES: MAENAD
AGE: OVER 8,000 YEARS OLD
STATUS: DEAD AND GONE
OCCUPATION: WORSHIPPER OF DIONYSUS

NOTES:

MARYANN FIRST APPEARED IN BON TEMPS AS A SOCIAL WORKER INTENT ON HELPING TARA AFTER A DRUNK-DRIVING INCIDENT. WE WOULD LATER FIND OUT SHE WAS IN FACT THE CAUSE OF TARA'S CAR ACCIDENT, AND NOT A REAL SOCIAL WORKER AT ALL. WITH HER OWN MINIONS EGGS, KARL, AND DAPHNE IN TOW, MARYANN LED A LAVISH LIFESTYLE, FEASTING ON TROPICAL FRUITS AND RATHER RARE MEATS. SHE WAS APPARENTLY CALLED TO THESE PARTS BY AN EXORCISM RITUAL PERFORMED ON TARA BY MISS JEANETTE, BUT THAT WASN'T HER ONLY CONNECTION: YEARS EARLIER, SHE CAUGHT A NAKED AND SCARED SAM MERLOTTE BURGLARIZING HER HOME. HE HAD RECENTLY BEEN ABANDONED BY HIS PARENTS, AND HAD NOWHERE TO TURN. SHE ENTICED SAM INTO HER BED AND TOOK HIS VIRGINITY, BEFORE HE STOLE OFF INTO THE NIGHT WITH A LARGE SUM OF CASH. WHEN SHE SURFACED IN BON TEMPS, MARYANN WASN'T INTERESTED IN GETTING THE MONEY BACK, BUT SHE WAS INTERESTED IN SACRIFICING SAM TO HER GOD. WITH THE FRENZIED CITIZENS OF BON TEMPS RALLYING BEHIND HER, BILL AND I HAD TO STEP IN TO RIGHT THINGS. WITH A LITTLE ADVICE I HAD PROCURED FROM THE DARLING QUEEN SOPHIE-ANNE, BILL HELPED SAM TRICK MARYANN INTO THINKING SHE HAD SACRIFICED HIM AND HER GOD HAD COME, LETTING HER IMMORTAL GUARD DOWN LONG ENOUGH FOR SAM TO IMPALE HER TO DEATH.

THE ROAD AHEAD

It's the beginning of a new year-January 14 to be exact. It has been a hard few months gathering evidence against vampires. I have witnessed things I could never have prepared myself for. I am exhausted, heartbroken over my split with Sarah, and at times, after witnessing so much evil, I have even questioned my faith. But I am reminded, time and time again, that I must hold on to hope. For if the devil exists, which we now have proof of, then that can only mean there is indubitably a God watching over us all. I trust in His plan to let the events of Armageddon unfold and I try to imagine all of the wonderful creations He'll be sending down to us to help win the war.

Satan may have vampires, but God has angels. Can you imagine how strong and beautiful they must be? Perhaps they are already walking alongside us, waiting to spring into action the moment things become darkest.

Like my father, I know that I have earned myself enemies while compiling my research and fighting the good fight. In fact, I can feel them closing in on me. I came back to my hotel in Dallas tonight to find it ransacked. Was it at the hands of vampires? Was it an act of humans? Was the room trashed by lizard men? I may never know, but I'm not sure I need to. It's time for me to get my life back together and settle things with Sarah. Perhaps tomorrow's pray-in will give me a chance to be surrounded by loved ones and congregants, and there I can ask God for help. For once these pieces are back in place, I will be ready to move on to PHASE 2: informing my followers-and the world-of my lessons.

Who knows? Maybe I'll even finish Daddy's book and publish all of this material.

In the end, I am just thankful that God has chosen me to be a key player in His grand opera. I will protect His children, wait for His angels, and accept whatever His next plan for me is with open arms.

Heaven, here I come!

KNOWN ENEMY

NAME: STEVE NEWLIN

SPECIES: VAMPIRE

AGE: 31 WHEN TURNED, STILL A "BABY VAMP"

STATUS: TURNCOAT

KNOWN RELATIVES: FATHER, THEODORE NEWLIN, EX-WIFE, SARAH NEWLIN.

OCCUPATION: SPOKESMAN FOR THE AVL (AKA THE NEW NAN FLANAGAN)/REVEREND

MAKER: UNKNOWN

KNOWN PROGENY: NONE

NOTES:
HAVING READ THROUGH STEVE'S FIELD GUIDE, I FIND IT NOTHING SHORT OF AMUSING THAT THE GREAT AND POWERFUL REVEREND NEWLIN IS NOW A VAMPIRE HIMSELF. IF YOU ASK ME, NAN WASTED HER PRECIOUS VAMPIRE BLOOD TO BRING THIS LOWLIFE SLIME OVER TO OUR SIDE. I WOULD HAVE JUST KILLED HIM . . . MAYBE ONE DAY HE'LL GIVE ME AN EXCUSE TO. IN THE MEANTIME, I'M HANDING THIS BACK OVER TO HIM. MAYBE OUR REVISIONS WILL OPEN HIS EYES TO A VAMPIRE'S TRUE NATURE.
SO STEVE, IF YOU'RE READING THIS, TAKE MY ADVICE AND PLAY NICE. YOU WOULDN'T WANT ME ON YOUR BAD SIDE.

THE SECOND COMING OF STEVE NEWLIN

Now that Mr. Northman has returned my old journal to me (albeit with some "changes") it seems only appropriate I should add an entry about the most important moment of my life, or I should say, afterlife.

I don't remember anything from the moment I was abducted from my car lo those many moons ago. The vampires that kidnapped me erased all memories of being taken. One minute I'm listening to my CD of "The Greatest Sermons of the 20th Century" and the next I find myself clawing my way out of six feet of cold earth.

At first I was disoriented, confused, terrified. I cried out for my mother, something I had not done since the year or two following her death when I was a boy. She did not answer. In fact, no one did.

Now, I have to cop to a little white lie I told Jason Stackhouse surrounding the advent of my turning. I told him my maker was a female vampire that abandoned me. That was a little teeny white lie I told him so he'd look at me and allow me to glamour him. The TRUTH is . . . I'm still not sure who my maker is. Before I could become accustomed to the brand new me, and discover the identity of my maker, I was hooded and chained with silver netting. My second-coming was a painful and violent one.

My kidnappers shuttled me by black helicopter from the deep, deep swamps in which I was born again to the Authority headquarters. My turning, it seems, had come from strict orders by Salome, who, upon our introduction, claimed it was as punishment for my bigotry and hatred against the vampire kingdom. Although I would later discover my true purpose was to be groomed as a replacement for Nan Flanagan (the Authority was growing increasingly tired of her tendency to display insolence), I was ushered to a dark chamber underground where I was kept hostage for months, subsiding on the very synthetic beverage I used to protest against while the rest of the world questioned my disappearance. During that time it was the thought of Jason Stackhouse that kept me from losing all faith.

I suppose there was some truth to what I told Jason. My maker did abandon me. He or she never came to check up on me. He or she never showed me any love. I learned to use my abilities from Salome and Nora and the council at the Authority. In many ways, I see the Authority as my maker. It was they who brought me over, gave me a new purpose and a second chance. Still I can't help but reflect upon the fact that like my human childhood, my vampire one has been colored by absent parenting. Maybe no one will tell me who my vampire daddy is because of all those hateful things I did as a human? The permanent sense of abandonment would be a worthy slap on the wrist, and it certainly forces me to display devotion to the council. I have to admit, it's a stroke of brilliance on their part.

For now, the mystery remains, and perhaps it will until I can prove myself a worthy and capable member of the vampire community. Fortunately I am now guided by one of the most charming, handsome and capable vampires in the world, Russell Edgington. And believe me, he just loves it when I call him Daddy.

Praise Lilith!

VAMPIRE STEVE

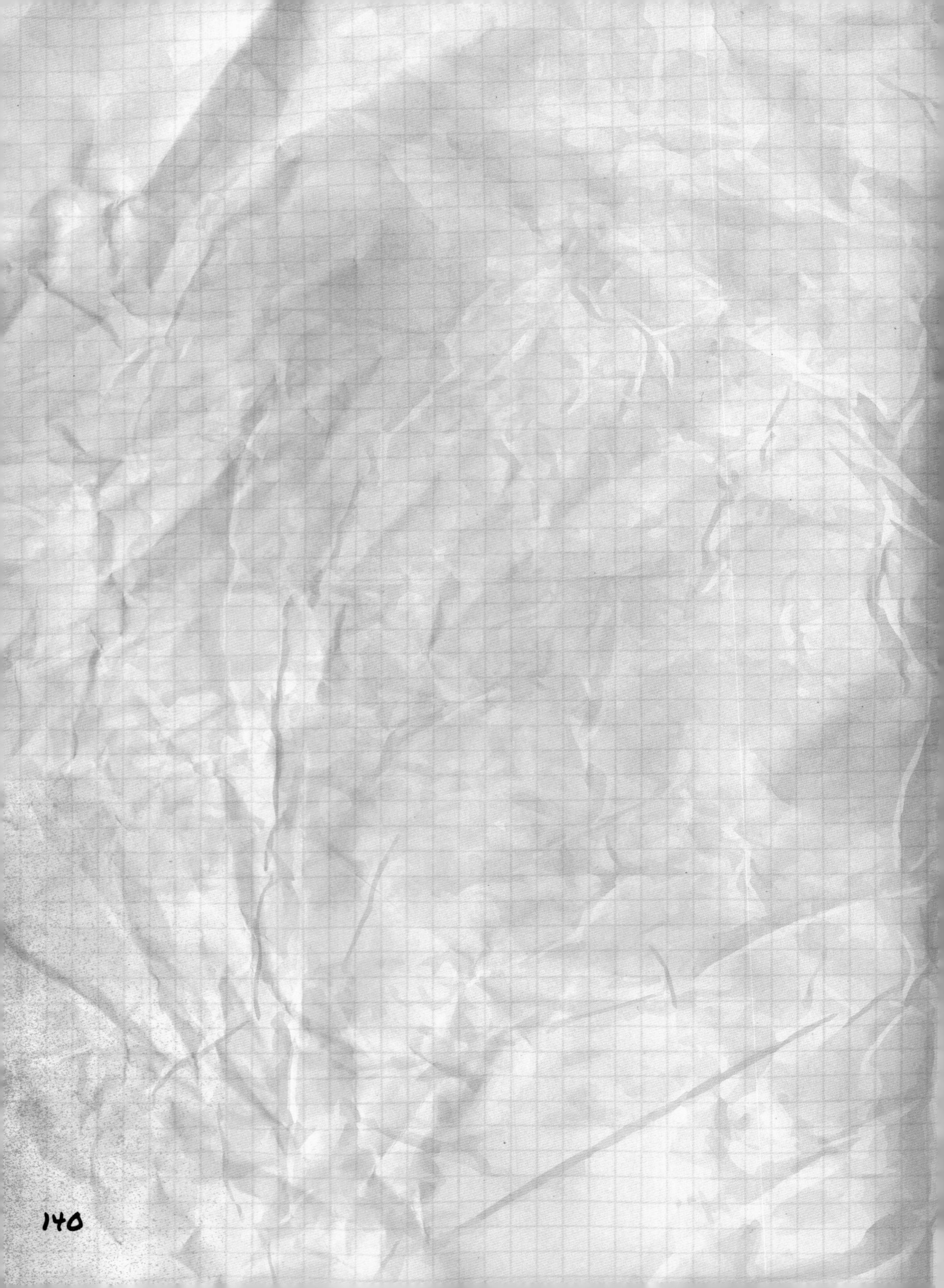

The authors would like to thank each other, for being so friggin' fantastic. Oh, and Charlaine Harris, for creating this awesome world and being the awesome lady that she is. We would also like to acknowledge the god formerly known as Alan Ball and his divine protege Christina Jokanovich, for their omniscience, omnipotence, and always refreshing vulgarity. These words could not have been written without the undying support of our drinking buddy, Sarah Malarkey. And these images could not have been illustrated without a gift of colored pencils from Lucy Griffiths, better known amongst *True Blood* fans as Nora, Eric Northman's bumptious sister. An additional thanks to Brian Buckner and Mark Hudis. And finally, Kim, thanks for letting us transform your dining room into a rent-free office.

Special Thanks To

James Costos, Stacey Abiraj, Josh Goodstadt, Janis Fein, Cara Grabowski, Robin Eisgrau, Tom Bozzelli, Suzuki Ingerslec, Cat Smith, and Tom Cahill.

IMAGE CREDITS/PHOTO CREDITS

True Blood series photographs by John Fleenor, Prashant Gupta, Doug Hyun, John P. Johnson, Steven Levine, Cat Smith, Gianna Sobol, Lacey Terrell, and Jaime Trueblood.

www.hbo.com

ILLUSTRATIONS
Cover and pages 7-10, 17, 20, 23, 41, 52, 55-57, 59, 60,
78, 79, 81, 83, 101, 110, 111, 115, 121, 123, 125-130, 132,
135 by Michael McMillian

Pages 26-27 and pages 62-63 by Lydia Ortiz
Page 70 by Kyle Hilton

Library of Congress Cataloging-in-Publication Data
available.

ISBN: 978-1-4521-2742-2

Manufactured in China
Designed by Michael Morris

10 9 8 7 6 5 4 3 2 1

Chronicle Books LLC
680 Second Street
San Francisco, California 94107
www.chroniclebooks.com

GIANNA SOBOL IS AN ASSOCIATE PRODUCER FOR *True Blood*. SHE LIVES IN LOS ANGELES, CALIFORNIA.

MICHAEL MCMILLIAN IS AN ACTOR, WRITER, AND ILLUSTRATOR WHO CURRENTLY PLAYS STEVE NEWLIN IN *True Blood*. HE LIVES IN LOS ANGELES, CALIFORNIA.